Dugan Holler

By Ann Robbins Phillips

Any names of people and similar events have been fictionalized and do not portray the actual and true happenings, especially in the local events of the time and place of the 1940's in Lawrence County, TN.

I am fascinated by our truly vibrant part of the state and country. The 1940's was a different time, and people thought and reacted differently than today. But they were who they were and tried to live as best they knew how. Oft times, their very livelihood was challenged in the wake of local drama and events. I challenge you to read about your history, your family...your ancestors. Get to know them. It has made us who we are today. Better yet, write the stories you know and have heard, and the events of your own life. Encourage others to do the same. Leave them at the Archives for future generations. In the voice of Amps from the first book of the REVENGE SERIES, "when their names are mentioned, they live again, if only for a few moments in time, in the heart of their families." Even those that we never met or knew.

---Ann Robbins Phillips

DEDICATION

I dedicate this book to M.C. and Lida Hooper Robbins, my parents. You bought and owned Dugan Holler for a time. It sat across the road from the house where I grew up, and it was the source of a few scary moments as a child when a panther (or whatever it was) screamed, and I shook like a leaf. It was a place of my nighttime dreams and my daytime enjoyment as I searched for leaves and insects for school projects. Although you would not recognize some of these stories, there are several that you would. You have left me with a love of family stories and scary ghost tales to last me a lifetime. I wish you were here to read the books and tell me your take on some of the personal accounts.

ACKNOWLEDGEMENTS

Thanks to the Lawrence County Historical Archives in Leoma for your help during some of the research of this book. My desire is that families write their histories and leave a copy in your safety. Generations that follow will thank you.

Thanks to Meagan Rouse, my great niece, my encourager, and helper. You and your daughter are in a line of strong women and family...you will carry on that line.

Thanks to my readers. You have encouraged me through the entire four books of this series. You let me blur the lines between truth and fiction and allowed me to call it factual fiction with tongue-in-cheek humor. I hope I have never disappointed you a single time. Without you, writing would be pretty useless. Your kind words and encouragement have kept me going. I love you all.

Thanks to family that have been by my side every step of the way. You read the books, tell your friends, and challenged me to keep on writing.

Chapter 1

Moving To Tennessee

Lottie hung her head out the truck window and filled her lungs with all the fresh mountain air she could take in. The trees danced in the gentle wind of the foggy morning and emptied drops of water from last night's rain on the hood. Beck reached out the window and grabbed a stick that fell on the windshield. She was certain the sun was already shining on the top of the mountain, but they were halfway up and a soft white cloud was forming as thick as pea soup. Lottie pulled her head back inside the truck and leaned her head against the door. She had hoped it would be a nice day when they left so she could see the houses of her loved ones as they passed. Then her wish had been to get on her knees and look out the back window as her beloved North Carolina and her family faded from view. Sometimes plans are just that...hopes that never happen. She'd said her good byes the night before when the family had gathered at Sugar's. Everyone had come to see them off. Everyone that was left, that is.

Lottie's Papa had died five years ago today. Nathe's funeral had been to his terms. His living family had gathered, and they had talked about all the good times they had when they were young and all living close to one another. He was laid to rest at the feet of his momma and papa. His Grandpa Amps was to his right.

Six months later, her Momma's funeral had garnished less tears. Not because they didn't love her as much as they did their Papa, but Addie had lost all will to live after Nathe had died. She was with him now, and it was what she wanted, planted to his left in the family section of the graveyard.

Life had passed by in a blink it seemed to Lottie. Yesterday, she was but a child playing in the mountains, hunting ginseng or gathering herbs with her Momma. Other than her family, she doubted she would have been able to recognize anyone she had grown up with. Smooth young skin had turned to wrinkles and her dark hair was gray and wiry. Sylva had grown into a lively town, and there were so many stores. Her first husband's family was dead, and the store they had owned was empty.

Lottie wondered if she'd ever see the mountains again. It didn't rightly matter. All she had to do was to close her eyes, and she was back. Like it used to be. With teams of horses and wagons. Smoke curling up from chimneys scattered across the mountain and into the valley. She could name the occupants of the houses in a twenty mile radius of her childhood home. She pictured herself on the seat in church by her Papa as the congregation sung, as the man up front chopped his hand in time with the rhythm of the music.

After her Papa had moved back, as a young man, to Jackson County from Newport, Tennessee, he had never again ventured beyond the rolling peaks of lower Appalachia. The mountains had been like a father to him. They had molded and marked him as their own. But to her, the draw of the mountains had always been where she had been born and grown up. Her ties to Jackson County, North Carolina were not to the land, but to the people, especially her Momma and Papa. Without them, the mountains meant nothing, and she found she didn't want to be there, even after all the years she had thought she did. In spite of its beauty, it was just dirt and trees and rocks and houses. Without a doubt, the only thing she knew she'd sorely miss was Sugar. Her baby sister's life was not what Lottie had hoped. Sugar had eight children and no husband. The change in her sister, and with her Momma and papa gone, had made it easier to move on to Tennessee like Beck wanted.

The farm had been divided, and her part of the land had been sold to her brother. That money, and what Beck and she had stashed away from him and the children working in the cotton mills, was enough to move to Tennessee. Her daughter, August, and her family were already there and begging them to hurry.

***

They left the mountains far behind, drove half way across Tennessee, and now had arrived in Lawrence County, Tennessee. Leaving behind the main road, they first passed a road to the left near a huge oak tree and then a narrow lane a half mile past that. At the third road they stopped. A sign had been written on a board and nailed to a post...Nubbin Ridge

Road. Beck turned and drove slowly down a packed chert roadway.

In spite of the hot sun beating down on the metal roof of the truck, Lottie felt a chill prickle over her body. She looked down at the flesh on her arms. It looked like a goose where she had plucked the down to put in a pillow, all bumpy and puckered. Her ears filled with a roaring sound. She leaned her head against the window and closed her eyes.

Norabell sat between Beck and Lottie. She felt the bumps on Lottie's arm rub against hers. "What's wrong, Momma?" Norabell rubbed her mother's bumpy arm.

"I have a feeling that I've been here before and driven down this same road. I feel like I know every inch of this land. It looks familiar. I'm sure I saw it in a dream when I was trying to decide if I thought it was a wise move coming to Tennessee."

"What else did you see? Was it good things or bad? Was any of it about me? Did I find some nice looking feller to marry?"

Lottie's body shook like a horse after he was given freedom from the saddle. "This road leads to a place. It lays to our right with thick trees and running water. I don't rightly remember all I dreamed, but it was meant for us to come here."

"Do you think there will be bad things happen while we are here?" Norabell's forehead wrinkled with concern.

Beck looked at them and shook his head. "Maybe I described it to you so good that you feel like you've been here. Or it could have been August that told you enough in her letters to make it feel familiar."

He knew better but knew this would rile Lottie.

"Hmphhhh. I don't think so. You wasn't here but a few days, and you had very little to say about it. Just that you thought I would like it in this part of Tennessee. You never mentioned any land for sale that you were interested in when you came back home to North Carolina. You don't know nothing about this land I saw. Poke fun all you want, but my spirit has been here before. It has walked these hills and hollers. There are people like you that don't want to hear such things...calling it nonsense. You should accept by now that I know what I'm talking about. There have been very few things of any importance that we have faced in life that I did not get a warning."

Lottie thought over events in her life when she was warned by something. A dream. A vision. A sign. There were unforgettable points, like death and people to be careful in her dealing with.

Lottie leaned her head against the back window of the truck and thought, *I'm glad that the good Lord never let me see more than a smidgen of things to come at any one time. It would have been unbearable. If a person looks up sorrow in one of them things called a dictionary I'm sure it would be my face for the whole world to see. But now I'm setting out to live a whole new life in Tennessee.* She remembered no second sight on anything it would bring; only how the land would look. But she had a good feeling deep inside her that things were going to be different. Good times.

Lottie reached down and rubbed her aching legs from sitting so long. They eased from the pain, and she sat up.

Norabell slid forward, laid her arms on the dashboard, and looked out the windshield. "Think real hard about what you saw in Tennessee, Momma, and see if I found a man. It's time I get married and have a home of my own. Maybe you saw his face. Was he a looker?"

"I told you that I don't remember all I saw right now. It'll come to me as I need it. As far as you getting married, you have plenty of time."

Beck slowed the truck. They stopped where a field covered in knee high corn ended at a stand of tall hardwood trees. "August said in the letter that she'd be at the road that leads to Dugan Holler. It's for sale, and she would point it out to us on our way. Then, we're to go to her house. She lives on Idaho Road."

Lottie saw August waving both arms in the air. "There she is. I knew this was the place even before you told me. I could feel it. Notice she is standing on the right side of the road. What did I tell you?"

August stepped up on the running board. "I was getting worried. Every day for the past week, I've come here and watched and waited all day long. I thought you'd get here earlier in the week."

Beck took off his hat and wiped his forehead. He smiled. "Coming over the mountains was hard on the brakes. And dangerous. I bought two sets of brake shoes before I left. It was a good thing. I had to use them both."

Lottie opened the door, and it pushed August off the running board and onto the ground. "I need to get out of this truck and stretch my legs. They're both asleep. I need to feel the ground under my feet." She took a step, and her body swayed.

August caught her under the arms and held her up. "Be careful. I don't' want you breaking no hip now that I have you here with me in Tennessee."

Lottie spread her legs to steady her wobbly body.

August looked at Beck. "We can't stay here very long. It'll be dark in a couple of hours. There's an old house next to us that Henry has fixed up for you all to live in until you can build a house if you want to buy the Dugan Holler. You can drive back and forth while you're cutting the timber. This would be close to us. I hope you buy this land."

"It sounds like you have already decided this is the place for us to purchase. Dugan Holler. It has a nice sound to it. If we stay here long enough, maybe they'll call it Radford Holler."

Beck put his hand on August's shoulder. "Your Momma swears she's been here before."

August bit her lip, then turned to Lottie and smiled. "You won't get me to deny she's seen it. Maybe in a dream. My Momma has gifts."

August turned back to the truck and rubbed her hand over the metal. "This is one fine automobile, Papa. I never thought I'd see you driving a truck. In my mind, I still see you driving a team of horses hitched to a wagon like it was when we were in Clifton or in Morganton."

"It seemed everyone is getting an automobile back in North Carolina. More cars than wagons for sure. It has come in handy to bring our possessions here."

Lottie still stood and stared at the trees.

Beck leaned forward and looked at Lottie. "Get in wife. We need to get on down the road."

August helped her Momma in then jumped on the running board. "I'll just ride right here. We can stop at the bottom of the hill and give the truck a wash when we ford the creek. Then we can go real slowly so it won't get dusty on the way home. I can't wait to see Henry's eyes when he sees this. We bought an old car, but he's not got it running yet. But he will. He's real handy with motors it seems." She looked at Lottie. "The land goes all the way to the bottom. The creek is the boundary. There is a house you can see on a rise above the creek. That's your nearest neighbor."

August kept chattering to her daddy. Lottie looked at the land as they coasted downhill in the truck. The land rolled gently, and it would be easy to log with a horse or mule.

They pulled onto the solid rock bottom of the creek.

Lottie stood back and looked at her neighbor's house. It was small but well built. "Who lives in that house?"

"Her family name is Flatwood. She's a widow with a couple of children...both older. I don't know her, but I did hear her son has left for the war. She appears to be a hard-working woman. I see her in the fields when I come by."

Lottie listened to Beck, August, and Norabell talk while they washed the automobile.

***

Henry came out as the truck pulled in front of the house. He whistled and rubbed his hand over the newly washed truck. "I bet you gave a pretty penny for this fine thing."

Beck's face lit up. "I got it at a great deal. It cost a bit more money than we thought we could spare, but it was worth it. We needed it to get here, and it'll be a great help on the farm. It's a 1939 Chevrolet. The man that owned it told us he had given $580 for it when it was new. Can you imagine anyone spending that kind of money on an automobile? He was the superintendent over one of the mills in Morganton. He could afford it." Beck put his hands on his hips. "I offered him $300. He said $400. I said $350. The rest is history. He tried to add on $2.50 for a rain wiper on Lottie's side of the truck, which is what he paid for one when he bought the truck new. I told him he could just take it off as Lottie wasn't doing the driving. I was. He kept pushing to make me pay for more extras he had purchased, like $2.55 for that mirror on Lottie's side. He talked about other extras like the rear bumper and road lamps. Even said because it was blue instead of black and he should charge more. I stuck to my guns...$350...and she's mine today. Lottie says I'm shifty-shifty."

They both laughed.

August sat down in the porch swing beside Lottie. "Ain't it just beautiful here Momma? The land is not so rough that you can't plant crops and make an easy living. There are hills and hollers but it's gentle rolling."

Lottie let her eyes drink in the strange land. She paused at each tree and noted its kind. Most were just like the ones in North Carolina. The wind blew the leaves and, at the sound, she closed her eyes and listened. "I don't hear another person talking, no motors running, and no fussing in houses nearby. It's heaven on earth."

August put her arm across the back of the swing and pulled her Momma to her. "I knew you would love living away from the city and those mill towns. Here, you can go any direction for quite a ways and not have to see anyone or listen to another voice unless you want to. People are real nice. This is our fifth spring season in Tennessee."

The swing slid back and forth as Lottie pushed her feet on the porch floor. "I always wanted a porch swing. We didn't dare spend a penny for anything extra for years. We were looking forward to moving to Tennessee. It makes it even nicer being you're here. I've missed you so much. We were always close. Especially after we lost the others. We're so much alike, August, you and me. We are both seers of things to come. Like me, you didn't always listen to those voices and feelings. You've made some mistakes, but look where you've come to now. God is good."

Tears came up in August's eyes. "Ever since the flood in Clifton, I hadn't seen much of the future until we talked about moving to Tennessee. There were no warnings of any kind. My mistakes were just mine. Without any help. And we've all paid the price."

Norabell stepped up on the porch. "What are you all talking about?"

"About you." August teased.

"What about me?" Norabell stuck out her tongue at August.

Lottie said, "About how you've gotten all grown up." She turned to August. "I was afraid that she would meet some feller and not come out here with us."

August winked at Norabell. "Oh, I wouldn't have worried about that. She has already been praying for some fine man to woo her when she got to Tennessee. I'm almost sure of it. It's every young girl's dream."

Norabell turned red. "Daddy is moving the truck over to that house and unloading our things. All but the tools he brought that he'll need to cut the trees on the land when we buy it. The land has to have lots of timber, he told Henry. Oh, and Henry said we're to spend the night here tonight."

"Momma, you sit right here in the swing and rest. I'll go help them unload. It won't take long. You don't have a lot. We'll see what we can come up with to fill the house from our extras."

Lottie didn't argue. This was the most peaceful she had felt in years, and she didn't want it to end. There would be time to have a much-needed conversation with August when everything was done.

Chapter 2

Neither Lottie nor Beck spoke as they left the truck by the road and walked the dirt wagon path toward Dugan Holler. August climbed out of the back to find that they had already walked a good ways ahead of her.

Beck took off his hat and pulled out the notes he had scribbled on a piece of paper when he talked to the man that was handling the sale. It told them to take the dirt road off of Nubbin Ridge Road, then to go to the left when it divided at a Y. The wider, right one, he said, led to houses up at the head of the holler. The first part of the road to the left was overgrown with bushes and small trees, but cleared as they went further. It was twisted with ruts made by heavy rains from the early spring, but it was still passable for a good truck.

"I thought they said the owners never built down here. Why is there a road?" Lottie made her way between the limbs.

Beck had never seen a better farm in his life. Maybe it was because it was finally a piece of land that would be theirs. Well, theirs and Aunt Nancy…Fi-Nancy, as he was known to say to anyone that spoke of the land. There was something about owning a piece of God's green earth that made a man feel rich. He stooped, reached out and raked back rock, leaves, and sticks and scraped up a handful of dirt. The aroma was rich and musty. It smelled like fresh rain after a drought.

He pushed the hat on his head. "Stay right here, Lottie. Let me check a few things."

She watched him go from tree to tree, stretch his arms around some and others he stepped off the width of the tree.

"The hardwoods are tall and straight. Some of the chestnuts are trying to die. I might need to cut those before the others. Maybe it will stop the blight from taking all of them out." An acorn fell from the oak and landed in front of him. "I'd need to cut timber to build a house and to make some money until we could start farming. But I want to make sure we replant. There'll be no clear cutting, except for farm land."

They continued down the hill with the only sound being the snapping of twigs under their feet. There was now very little undergrowth due to the lack of sunlight from thick, heavy leaves. It made it easier to walk.

Beck stopped. "We'll not go to the bottom today. We'll save that for another time."

"Look at that one there." Lottie pointed at a tree across from them. The tree was tall and so large that he and Lottie together, hand to hand, could not reach around it.

Lottie turned to Beck. "There are houses already built and waiting, you know."

She walked down the path a little ways and stared through the trees. "They're down there sitting by the stream. I saw them in a dream. They're not much to look at, but we can make them livable until we can get the land cleared for farming. We can still cut the lumber to build us a real nice house."

August had caught up with them. She walked up to Lottie's side. "Houses are not possible, Momma. They said this land has been owned by the same people for over seventy-five years, and nobody ever lived on it. It was bought by the Cincinnati German Catholic

Tennessee Homestead Association Christian when they bought up land here for their people to move down from Ohio."

Lottie kept staring down the path. "Maybe it was a squatter. I don't' know why or who, but those buildings are down there. I'm going to that stream I can hear running. It won't take us much longer to check it out."

August turned around and shrugged her shoulder at Beck. "What can I say? She's usually right about things like this. I saw the house we bought in a dream before we got here. Momma has second sight. I got it from her. I'd put my money on the fact that she knows more than we do." She put her hand on Lottie's arm.

"Momma, I want you to live in the house we fixed up until you move. You will be close to me."

"We might do that. If we're able to buy this, they may need fixing up anyway. I want to walk every inch of it before I say yea or nay. We have some of the money. Any borrowing will mostly be for the sawmill. Even though I've seen it all in a dream, I need to make sure that everything feels right. But something inside me says this land is ours!" Lottie said as she kept walking down toward the creek.

Beck and August followed her down the wagon road and to the base of the holler. There sat the two houses right by the stream...just like she had described them. She turned and stared at Back.

Beck reached for her hand and smiled. "You were right. Do I need to say anything else?"

She really wanted to say *I told you so*, but instead followed as they climbed back to the top of the hill.

Lottie was winded about halfway up. She gasped, then stopped to catch her breath. She reached down and rubbed her calves. They were throbbing. She'd be sore tomorrow.

She laughed and said to Beck and August. "It's all I dreamed and more, but I sure do need to get used to climbing hills on a regular basis."

"I'll have Henry drive into town in the morning and make an appointment at the bank where you can borrow the rest of the money you need. The newspaper said Commerce Union Bank was offering some choice farm property. This is on the list. They said they were going to dispose at prices that would mean real buys for those who take advantage of it."

Beck smiled. "I'll go with him."

August shook her head. "You can stay here and help set up the house. He has a meeting after that. He joined the Home Guard, and they'll meet in town tomorrow night. The group has 47 men in it already. They have equipment coming in, and they'll begin to instruct them on how to use it. I'm so proud of him."

Lottie turned one last time and surveyed the land with her eyes.

***

Lottie watched Beck twist his hat around and around in his hands as he listened carefully to the banker. He explained what they were going to sign that day. It was the papers that would allow them to borrow the money to buy the land and enough extra to buy a small sawmill so they could cut the trees in Dugan Holler. She watched the banker write down the address on Nubbin Ridge Road. The paperwork seemed complicated. She didn't understand the ins and outs of the loan, but she trusted Beck. Finding ways to pay it back was where she could help. She could pinch a nickel until the buffalo squealed.

She looked out the window and began to daydream. One day, they had walked almost every square foot of the land. She'd noticed how the trees covered the holler and ridge on the back side as thick, if not thicker, than on the front. They were huge. Virgin timber, no doubt. Beck had explained that he would first cut the timber where the house would be built to make a place for the house to set.

They had walked the entire back edge and turned down into the holler. She'd smiled as she pointed out again that the houses had been just like she'd seen in her dream. They could be made liveable with just a little fixing up. Maybe not made for the winter, but she was sure Beck would have the house built by then.

She jumped when the banker called her by name. Both men stared at her blank look.

"I'm sorry. My mind was a hundred miles away." Lottie put her hands to her mouth.

The banker smiled. "That's fine. I was just asking you if you were completely behind your husband purchasing this property and buying this sawmill. As I told him, I've seen many a wife take a teaspoon and throw out the money a man earns faster than he can shovel it in."

Lottie laughed. "It's fine with me. We'll pay back every last cent. I raised a family while having to watch every dime we earned. This is a fine farm. In fact, I've been here before..."

Beck turned bright red. "Lottie. You answered his question. Me and him needs to move right along and get these papers signed. He told me about somebody that might want to sell a small sawmill. That will help us save a ton of money." He waved to Lottie to stand up and come to his side. "Sign right there...right below my name."

Lottie followed Beck and watched him put on his hat. He touched it lightly at a man that crossed in front of them.

They had barely gotten out of the man's office before another gentleman brushed by them. "I heard that Dugan Holler is for sale."

Lottie bit her lip and tried not to laugh. "Let's get out of here. That farm is ours. We barely got here in time. Of course, I knew we would. It was meant to be. Some things are in God's plan, and this is one of them."

They stepped onto the street, and Beck grabbed Lottie's hand. "About what happened in there...I don't think I'd be telling people about your second sight. August told me she warned a person that lived down the road from her after she had a dream about them, and it happened just like she said. She thought they'd be grateful, but they spread a rumor she was a witch. She keeps it to herself now. You might want to do the same."

Lottie looked at the people walking in both directions in front of them. "If you think that's best, I'll try to keep it to myself. When I tried that before, it got where I never saw things for the longest time. In some ways that might be nice, but since we come here, all I feel is that things are going to be good. I want to keep that feeling. We've had a long season of hard times and heartache. The hope of a better life feels mighty fine to me."

Beck shook his head. "Feelings are one thing. I'm talking about telling people about your second sight. If we want to fit in here, we need to not be talking about our mountain ways. All those superstitions need to be kept to yourself. No stopping blood. No blowing out fire or taking off warts. Don't be warning people of things that are going to happen to them."

Lottie wrung her hands. "I don't know if I can do that, Beck. If someone knew something bad was going to happen to me, I'd want them to say something. Wouldn't you? It didn't make us enemies in Clifton or Morganton. People were nice to me."

"They were to your face."

Lottie turned red. "What do you mean? Was I talked about?"

Beck slipped his hand behind her and guided her to the truck. "I don't know. I guess I'd want to know something if I could change it. But if you want to fit in and have a new start on life, you might want to find a way to not be so open with your 'gifts'. Feel people out and see if you think they would take kindly to it. Just be careful. We're going to live here until we die. I want our last days to be happy."

"I will be happy. Happy is a choice. It doesn't depend on what others do, at least not for me."

Lottie thought about how she had carefully signed the papers and how Dugan Holler was theirs. Everything felt right to her. If she had her way, she'd be buried on the hill behind the house they planned to build in the holler. People could talk if they liked. She could only be the person she was. If they didn't like her, it wouldn't be any skin off her nose.

Lottie would have nothing but for them to stop by the land on their way home. She jumped out of the truck like a young girl. She fell on her knees and kissed the earth. "You're ours, Dugan Holler. We'll make you the best farm in all of Lawrence County."

Beck laughed, but his face softened as she looked like the old Lottie from years ago. She no longer had the slower gait of the old woman she'd become. Owning the farm and knowing the work ahead had made her feel young. He knew she was in heaven. Every day of the two weeks they'd been in Tennessee, she'd come in August's wagon or talked him into driving her to the farm in the truck. Her feet had walked the entire edge of the parcel of land while she cried and prayed for it to be hers. God must have heard her cries. It was about time for laughter. Troubles and sorrows were about all they'd seen for years. All the hard work and sacrifice was paying off now. They owned land! They could work in the fresh air and not fill their lungs with the lint from the cotton mills.

***

For three days, Lottie and Norabell had walked from Idaho Road to where Beck and Henry was cutting logs. Each time, two women had passed in front of them at the place where the road to Dugan Holler crossed the wider path that led to the land beyond. An old woman was dressed in what appeared to be three layers of colorful skirts and an embroidered vest. A dark scarf covered her head and was tied tightly beneath her chin. She was in the company of a young woman that looked to be in her early twenties, hair in a braid that hung to her waist. The younger held the older woman's arm and guided her along. They passed a little closer each day than the day before.

Today, the older woman stopped and looked directly at them. Both stared back into her darks eyes which shot arrows of unease into the heart of Lottie.

The old woman walked to Norabell's side and grabbed her hands. She pried loose Norabell's tightly squeezed fingers. The woman ran her finger down each line on her hand, raised her right arm, and cupped the young girl's face with her long, slim fingers. "Your wedding will be not many days hence. It will be a good match, but fate will plaque your life with strange happenings, especially early." The woman took a deep breath and leaned her face close to Norabell's and stared into her eyes. "I see two women, both are dressed in black and their face is covered with veils. One of the women has red on her dress." The old woman jumped back. "Blood!"

The woman raised her chin and looked down her nose at Lottie. "When you pry, it will take you to evidence you did not plan to find. It does not tell the whole story. There are things on which it will not enlighten." She laughed deeply in her throat.

Her eyes glanced sideways at Lottie who had her hand over her mouth. She turned back and pointed her long, bony finger at Norabell. "You will be brought to a dark time in another's life. You will question everything you've been told." She stopped for a moment but never took her eyes from Norabell. "Be careful the place you choose to live...for where the bird doth fly, the man will die, in anger he hath left in gall, there his spirit again may call."

She turned her back to them and stared in the direction from which she had come. With that one turn, she had dismissed them.

The younger woman smiled slightly at Norabell's red face, then dropped her eyes. "We are Roma."

The older woman grunted and grabbed the younger's arm and pulled her along the path. They returned in the direction they had come. It was strange, as all other days they had continued on their way.

"Lordy, you're as white as a sheet." Lottie grabbed Norabell's arm and pulled her to a tree. "Lean here until you get your legs back."

"Who was that woman?" Norabell whispered.

"A better question might be **what** was that woman."

"Fine. Then, what was that woman."

"The tree is not enough." Lottie motioned her shaking daughter toward a stump and helped her to sit down. "She was a gypsy, no doubt. Or Roma as the younger suggests they are called. She told your fortune without so much as asking for a chicken or a ham." Lottie looked in the direction the two had left.

"I ain't never seen a real live gypsy before. People at school talked about them. I want to know how there can be a wedding when I ain't met no man since I've been here. As for the other she spoke about, there ain't been no time to make any friends, what with cutting trees and clearing up the brush from the trimmings. I'll never remember all she had to say. Do I need to know it?"

Lottie pulled her eyebrows together. "I'm not sure what to make of a gypsy. My Momma would not have let me go to one, and I don't plan on starting now. They use cards, and I don't believe in that or the use of crystal balls. That is, if they really use those like I hear. In life, I figure that anything that has a counterfeit, it must have a real. I see things and know things before they happen. To me, it comes from God. I've never asked a gypsy where her powers come from, so I can't rightly say. It seems that I'm not in a position to judge. As far as if she is true about what she says about your future, we'll just have to wait to see if it comes to pass. Then we will visit this time in our mind and see if we can figure it out." She smiled at Norabell. "I'll remember the words she said."

Norabell said, "It can't be true. I don't know a soul here."

Lottie left Norabell's whiney voice and walked to the log road that the gypsy women had walked away on. She kicked leaves and moved scattered, small limbs where paths of wheels would have been. "I wonder where she's living. There's not been a wagon or automobile down this road in quite some time." Lottie stooped. "Maybe a horse in the past week." She stood up and took a few steps down the road. "A feeling keeps coming to me that this woman will come back into our life for some reason."

She turned and waved for Norabell to get up and come with her. "Let's hurry. Your Papa is expecting us. He'll be back with the lumber he took to be run through the planer in Leoma until we find out if the sawmill we bought has a plane with it. It'll be here in a few weeks.

We'll help unload, and then the men can start building our new house."

***

At the bottom of Dugan Holler, they stopped and scooped up water with their hands. "I'll bring a dipper tomorrow and hang it here near the place we ford the creek so we can get a proper drink."

Norabell sat down on the creek bank. "Remember us talking about how you saw this place before we come. Then, this gypsy woman said I'd get married real soon. How come you both see things out in the future, and I have to wait for things to happen to know anything?"

Lottie smiled at Norabell's sullen face.

"Momma, are you sure you didn't see some man at my side in your dream or vision? Was he maybe tall and handsome, and have hair that curls over the top of his ears? Does he have a pretty little sorrel mare that he was driving to a little cart when he came a-courting?"

Lottie looked down at Norabell's soft face. "Have you seen something yourself? You seem to know a lot about some man? Either that, or you got it all planned. It might not happen like you think. You need a good man, but you can't always be so choosy as to the way his hair curls."

Norabell put her hand to her mouth and turned bright red. "Well, actually, August told some young man all about me. He goes to their church. They had just moved to Leoma from Ohio. He came back and asked Henry for my mailing address. He wrote me a letter, and I happened to get the mail one day while you were gone. After that, I told him to write me and send it to one of my friend's address. We've been courting by mail for near onto a year. He sent me a picture." She reached down into her bosom and pulled out a piece of newspaper. She carefully unfolded the worn paper and brought out the picture. She handed it to Lottie.

Lottie looked from Norabell to the picture and back to her. "And you didn't think this was something you should've talked to me about?"

Norabell folded her arms and stared. "What was the matter with me writing to a young man? I'm seventeen years old."

"You would've been sixteen then. The point is that, if you kept it a secret, there must have been some reason."

Norabell wrinkled her nose. "I didn't know if I wanted to court a man by letter. I like to look them in the eye when I talk to 'em. See if they are telling the truth if they say they like me. If they're nearby, I could ask my friends and find out if they were two-timing me. I couldn't do that by letter. I figured it would be a note or two, and it would be all over. It didn't happen that way. He wrote two times a week, every week. After about three months, I didn't say nothing because I didn't think I would ever get to see him in the flesh. But when you started talking about moving out here, I knew it might happen. This might be the man for me."

"Why didn't you tell me then?" They walked toward a shallower place in the creek where they could step on the rocks to cross.

"Well...then my mind got to reasoning that when he saw me, it might all be over. I never had a picture to send him. I probably don't look like he thinks I do. If he says it's off, then I wouldn't have to explain to everyone it was because I was ugly."

Lottie stopped and grabbed Norabell. "You're about the prettiest thing around here. What makes you think you're ugly?" She pulled her to the water's edge and pointed at her reflection. "Look at that beautiful curly red hair. There are girls that would kill for your looks. Your face is smooth, and you don't have freckles, in spite of working in the sun. The bonnet helps, but it never has benefitted me or August. We're both freckled-faced."

Norabell grabbed Lottie and gave her a tight hug. "Thank you, Momma. I know you think I'm pretty. I just hope he does. I'm glad somebody in our family in the past had good skin for me to get. This red hair I could've done without." She laughed and skipped from rock to rock as she crossed over the water.

Chapter 3

Norabell waited until the sun was an hour away from sinking into the west before she came to where her Momma sat on the front steps with her feet ankle deep in a pan of water.

"Momma, I'm going to pick dewberries in the ditch by the road. I'll be back before dark."

Lottie rubbed a rag on the cake of lye soap and wiped the mud that had formed on her dusty feet when she put them in the water. "Lordy, child, you should've done that this morning if you wanted a berry pie for tonight's supper."

"It's fine.   We can cook them down to dribble over the biscuits in the morning." Norabell said but didn't look her Momma in the eyes.

"Hurry back. As soon as my achy, dirty feet get clean, and they cool off a bit in the water, we need to start supper. Your Daddy will be as hungry as a bear. He ain't had a bite since noon when I carried a pot of soup to him and Henry."

The last words were yelled at her daughter's back.

* * *

Norabell had timed it well. The girl with the charcoal-colored hair she'd seen yesterday met her where the paths crossed.

"Hello. You're the one that was with the older woman I saw yesterday. Right?"

The girl didn't smile. "I am. What do you want?"

Her words stung. "I don't want anything. I thought you were about my age and, since I'm new here, we might become friends."

"You want to be my friend? Really?" She turned to walk away.

Norabell ran after her. "I don't have any friends here. You could introduce me to the neighbors. Do you have brothers and sisters?"

She stopped and turned around. "You ask a lot of questions but don't wait for an answer."

There was a possible smile on the girl's lips. Norabell took a deep breath. "That's what my family says all the time. With you, I was afraid if I didn't ask fast, you'd be gone before I could finish."

"You're funny. If I was gone, I wouldn't answer any of them, anyway."

Norabell laughed. "That's true. I didn't think of that. My name is..."

"Norabell. I heard your Momma call you that yesterday. It's a pretty name."

"Thank you. What's your name?" Norabell sat down on a stump and hoped she would do the same.

She leaned her back against a tree across from Norabell. "They call me PeNellie or just Nellie. My name is Penelope Walachia but we say our surname is Welch. It's easier that way."

Norabell watched PeNellie as she talked, and she looked in the direction that Norabell suspected her family lived...the head of Dugan Holler. "My Momma said you are gypsies. Are you?   And that woman with you was your granny?"

She smiled. 'My Mamia. Yes. She was the one that told your future. We are Roma."

The root was uncomfortable, and Norabell stood. "Roma. I'll have to talk to you about that later, how does your grandmother, your Mamia, know my future?"

"Roma are well known for telling people their future. My Papa hates it when she does that.   Although we're Roma, we've left the others of our clan. Papa says if we are to stay here and make it our home, we must try to fit in. We want to settle, to stay here for a long time."

"My Momma can tell the future too. Well...sometimes she can. She has dreams or 'visions' as she likes to call them. But she can't do it whenever she wants to. They seem to come to her at strange times. Like a warning that something is going to happen. And then it does."

PeNellie glanced at Norabell as they walked.

Norabell slowed down only a tiny bit then asked, "Does she get money for telling people's fortune?"

She overlooked the question. "We came here in our vardo, our wagon. We rented a house that you reach by the way of this path. Papa asked Mamia not to tell fortunes. She said if he could play music then she could surely be able to use her gifts as well." PeNellie laughed. "It doesn't matter what he says. Mamia will do as she pleases. She's very good at what she does. She's hardly ever wrong." She raised her eyebrows at Norabell. "Are you planning a wedding?"

Norabell bit her lip and turned red. "Only in my mind. He doesn't know a thing about it yet. In fact, I've never laid eyes on him. We've been courting with letters back and forth from North Carolina to here. I'm afraid he'll not want me once he sees me. His picture shows that he is nice looking. I'm plain compared to him."

"You're not plain looking. You are quite unforgettable. That red hair alone makes you extraordinary. You look nothing like your Momma. It must be your Papa that gives you such a striking look."

Norabell waved her hand. "It must be in my family further back than I know anyone. There's not a red head in the bunch."

PeNellie stood up straight and pushed stray hairs away from her face. "We can meet here sometime if you like. You can let me know about this man that you plan on marrying.

Sometimes, I come to meet the peddler alone. You could find me then, if you want."

"I'd like that. If your Mamia says anything else about me, let me know."

She put her hand on Norabell's shoulder. "Don't get me wrong. I love my Mamia, and she does know things that others do not. But do not live your life waiting on others telling you what will happen. Know what you want, then go after it. That's all a person needs to do to break away from a history of troubles in a family. Your grandfathers may have killed and feuded their entire lives, but it does not have any effect on your life unless you let it."

She remembered her Momma telling her about the history of her family. She stared at PeNellie. *How does she know this?* She wondered.

"We will meet any time you like. Just come here. I'm not like Mamia, but I will know inside that you're here and will come to you. True friends have a bond...or so I heard." Her hand dropped from Norabell's shoulder, and she ran through the woods.

Chapter 4

Norabell sat in her usual place in the truck, between Lottie and Beck. She gathered her dress into her fist, then she'd let go and smooth it out over her thighs.

"Stop it Norabell. You're going to ruin that dress before we get to church. I know you're nervous about meeting this young man, but messing up your clothes is not the right way to make a good impression."

Norabell looked at Lottie with tears in her eyes. "Do you really think he'll like me?"

"My goodness. I think he'll love those big, beautiful eyes and pretty smile. Just be yourself. Don't get all wound up and trip over your words. Slow down and act real lady-like. It looks like from his letters that he already knows all about you."

Norabell's eyes widened like huge saucers. "You read my letters? Why would you do that?"

"Hmph. Do you think I don't want to know all about the young man that thinks he's in love with my Norabell? You'd do the same if you had a daughter. I found them after you told me about him. They were in your belongings when I was putting them away at the house." Lottie continued talking while Norabell shook her head to disagree. "Yes, you would. Come back to me in about seventeen years and tell me all about it, baby girl. I promised to take care of you as best I can, and this is one way I'm keeping my promise. It has actually made me somewhat fond of the young man. He has a good, legible handwriting and can spell well. I want you to have somebody that'll take you far in life. His grammar is good, and he seems very polite as best as I can tell by the things he writes."

Norabell hugged herself and smiled. "I'm just praying he likes me after he sees me."

Beck looked over her head at Lottie and smiled. "I wondered why you were all gussied up. I know that this young man had better treat my girl right, or I'll hunt him down and make him wish he had."

"Oh, Daddy!" Norabell squealed but grinned from ear to ear.

***

Beck had driven slowly so as to not stir up dust and make the truck dirty. He tended to that truck like it was a newborn baby. He washed it at least once a week.

August was waiting for Momma, Daddy, and Norabell outside the door of the church. She attended Idaho Church. It was a little white church down the road from where she lived. People were filing through the front doors. There were several young people near what appeared to be a spring, passing a dipper one to another with water to drink. One of the young men tossed the last of the water in the dipper at the feet of a girl near him. She pretended to run toward him, and he ran to the other side of the spring.

August motioned for them to hurry inside to sit with her and Henry.

Beck took off his Sunday-go-to-meeting hat at the door and led them down the aisle. Norabell sat down between August and Lottie. Up front, a woman sat down at the piano and played a few notes. August handed them songbooks and whispered, "We all sing by the shape of the note here. They have singing school twice a year if you want to learn. It's a real nice sound."

Lottie raised her eyebrows at Beck when he spoke louder than August had. "Hmmph. I've always sung by the letter. Open up and let 'er fly."

A red-faced August glanced around. Those in front of them had heard his reply and laughed.

It was then that Norabell saw him. *Jacob!* Her heart did a belly flop inside her chest. He was at the end of the row of those laughing, his arm draped over the seat behind his little sister.   He turned and stared straight at Norabell.   Her face was hotter than a late summer wash day, and just as red as the sunset. She grabbed her belly and leaned back. Her eyes were locked with his.   Then, he winked at Norabell. She smiled and bowed her head.   He'd ended every letter to her by drawing two eyes, one closed in a wink.

He sat with his arm up on the seat the whole service and would sneak a peek at Norabell when he thought no one was looking. During the closing prayer, she looked up to find him smiling at her. She caught her breath. He was more handsome in person. The sound was enough that Lottie raised her head, looked from one to the other, and frowned. They both shut their eyes quick. Her Momma acted tough, but she opened her eyes again just in time to catch a smile on Lottie's lips.

***

Norabell slipped away from the others and walked to the spring. There was a light cough behind her, and she turned.

"I had never even seen a picture of you, but I knew it had to be my Norabell the minute you walked in the door of the church."

She bit her lip and lowered her face. Jacob reached out and brushed her hair away from her face, then lifted her chin. Her eyes met his and he smiled.

"What happened to that chatty young lady that could write two pages of paper, front and back? Has the cat got your tongue?"

Norabell pulled away from his hand. "You look even better than your pictures," she mumbled.

He laughed loud enough that others looked in their direction. Norabell blushed.

"Why would you never send me a picture so I could dream about you?"

She sat down on a tree stump. "We didn't make many pictures, and the only one I had was when I was fourteen. You would've had nightmares if I'd sent you that one. I looked about eleven. It was taken by a man that came and took pictures of people that worked in the textile mills. I didn't work there, but I played along the river when my chores were caught up. He brought it back when he visited the next time."

"I'd like to see it. I bet you were pretty as a child, too."

"Then you'd lose that bet. I've never been pretty."

Beck came to a yelling distance and called to Norabell to come on. They were going to August's house for dinner.

She stood and Jacob walked closer to her. "You're very wrong about you not being pretty. I think you're beautiful. Your sister lives near me. I might drop by for a visit this afternoon. That is, if you'd like for me to."

"I think that would be fine. My Daddy and Momma will get to meet you." She wrinkled her nose, and he smiled.

Norabell looked toward where the horses and wagons were tied. Beyond that were several cars and trucks. "Where is that little cart and sorrel mare you talked about in your letters?"

He smiled and turned around. 'It's there. So you remember that?

"I remember about everything you wrote to me. You can come for that visit in that cart and take me for a ride."

"I'll be glad to meet your family, but it's you I want to see. We already know each other better than lots of young couples do before they get hitched. We were more forthcoming in letters than most people are face to face. This may be a short courtship in people's eyes."

Her throat felt tight. She tried to swallow, but her throat was dry.

"Come on, Norabell. We're waiting." Beck walked closer to where they stood.

Norabell ran as fast as her feet could carry her. She wasn't sure, but she thought he had just hinted about them someday marrying...the first day they had laid eyes on each other. *Surely I'm wrong!* She kept going over and over about what he had said.

Chapter 5

A light rain had been falling steady since daybreak.   The leaves had held all they could and now dripped with the misty rain. Lottie had stayed home. Norabell dreaded working in rain.

Norabell would pile brush as Beck cut it from the trees. August and her husband were helping, too. Henry worked in town but had taken the day off to help them. Lottie would have supper when the others got home tonight.

Beck handed a coat to Norabell and opened the door to the truck. "Put that on.

It'll only keep out the water for a spell. By then, you'll have worked up a sweat anyway and won't care that you're wet. I'm going to leave the truck at the road. If the rain picks up, we might get it stuck in the holler. We can walk out."

None of them spoke until the fork of the road that led off to the right toward where Penelope lived. It has been several days since Norabell had seen her. She considered letting Penelope's Mamia Welch tell her whole fortune and see if she mentioned anything worthwhile. But she didn't have money of her own.

She stopped to retie her shoes so she could stall for time. This was the time of the day Penelope left to trade eggs to the peddler that brought wares and foods in his truck once a week. It worked.

"Hi Penelope." She yelled at the two coming up the hill. Norabell ran to meet her friend, and they stopped. Mamia Welch walked further to where Beck was standing.

The two girls watched Mamia and Beck, and Norabell forgot everything she had planned to say to Penelope.

"What do you think they're talking about?" Norabell asked.

"I don't know, but my stomach gets fluttery when she's beyond where I can hear her." Penelope turned her head slightly as she tried to listen.

"Norabell, we need to get on down to the holler." He yelled. "August and Henry are too far ahead of us to know we stopped. They won't know what happened to us."

"I want to say hello. I haven't seen Penelope for two weeks. It won't take but a minute.' She shouted back.

Mamia Welch walked closer and stood beside Beck. "I can tell your fortune if you like. It won't cost you much."

Beck pulled his work hat low over his eyes and looked at her. He put his fingers together and tapped them for a moment. He reached in his pocket and handed her a coin.

She put it in her pocket and smiled. "Give me your hand." She looked down at his hand for a bit, and then put her hands around his. "You're a very lucky man. You have a good family. The land you have bought will bring you much fortune. The barn in the holler has a hidden room. Inside it, someone has hid money. It is yours. The people who left it are gone away, never to return."

Beck jerked his hand back. "I've been all through that barn. There's no hidden room. I would have noticed it right away."

The old lady jerked her hand away like she was burned. "Have it your way. It don't matter to me."

"Let's go, Norabell. We need to work a while before the rain picks up so much that we have to go home." Beck walked down the hill at a brisk pace.

Norabell ran back to the old woman and turned her red face to her. "I'm sorry."

"It is no skin off my nose. If he wants to believe, it can help him. If not, that's fine with me."

"You told his fortune?" Norabell looked at her daddy's red face.

"I did," she said.

"I want to talk to you, but Daddy will be mad if I don't leave right now. I have questions. I will try to get money."

Beck yelled over his shoulder. "Come on Norabell. I'm leaving."

The old woman reached and wiped the rain from the face of the young girl that stood in front of her. "You do not need to ask me anything. At this time, I cannot tell you more than you already know. The rest will come in good time. My advice is to think a long time but speak only a short time. Much can be learned if you're quiet. About the things that trouble you, you must know there were unforeseen circumstances...even before you were born. All things were done with good intention. It is important for you to talk to your family...after you have, think through all that you learn. Take your time."

"How do you know the things to tell me? I've not told you anything."

"My child, I know all things." She laughed and walked away with Penelope.

"I'm coming, Daddy." Norabell ran through the rain that had picked up considerably, sliding on wet leaves and plants. She caught up with Beck as they got to the barn.

"There's some brush from yesterday. Take it to the pile I started down by the branch. We'll burn it when the weather dries up. I have something I need to do." Beck left and went to the barn.

He climbed into the loft and walked around all four sides. There was daylight between each board. *No hidden room!*

The stalls were the same. In the room where the tack was kept, his eyes glanced toward one wall that should have had the same light streaming in. The cracks were dark with no sunlight sifting through. *Is this where the room is?* He tried to peek between the wood but he couldn't see anything. Now, he knew what the Welch woman had spoken was true. This afternoon, after he took Norabell, August, and Henry back to the house, he'd come back and bring Lottie with him. If he couldn't find a door, he'd make one with an ax. He wondered if it could be true that there was a fortune behind those walls.

Beck felled a few trees. Henry took a hand saw and cut off limbs while Norabell and August piled the brush. The rest of the day, Beck set up the gasoline saw mill that he had bought and the former owner had delivered the day before. It would make their work faster. If only the war would hold off or could be won quickly. There was already talk of rationing gas. It could hinder their progress. There was a field that had been cleared at the back of the place. He had talked to some about using corn liquor to run the motor, if rationing became a way of life. He might not should tell Lottie that it was liquor. All she had to know was it was homemade gasoline from corn. Beck smiled to himself.

***

Beck and Norabell, followed by Henry and August, crossed the path where they had met the two women and, this time, saw their backs disappear out of Dugan Holler as they swiftly returned home.

It had rained heavier on the main road than in the holler, and the roads were rutted from the automobiles that had passed during the day. The trip home took longer than usual. At one time Beck had moved so far to the side to let another car meet him that he had almost gotten stuck. The back end of the truck swished back and forth as he applied more gas.

"I guess I'll be washing the truck on the way to work in the morning." Beck smiled at Norabell. "And I guess you can help me."

Norabell laughed. "You love this truck more than you love me or Momma. I've not seen you one time wash Momma up when she gets dirty helping you."

Beck threw his head back and laughed. "You think so, do you? Well, I have you know your Momma did not cost as much as this truck. It's a known fact that you take better care of things when you have to pay a lot for them."

"I don't like you saying that. Momma works hard. She helps you make money, and she hardly ever spends any.   And when she does, it's never on herself."

Beck's face softened. "I'm just teasing you. I value your Momma more than the truck. She's just plenty capable of washing herself. "

They both smiled.

"Norabell, if you're as good a wife as your mother, you'll make one man very happy."

She scooted close to her daddy and planted a kiss on his cheek.   "Thank you, Daddy. I'll tell Jake you said so."

"Jake, hmmm. Is he one you think you'll marry? He needs to remember he has to ask for your hand from me, and then I have to agree. He might not be good enough for my little Norabell...my little ding-a-ling."

"Oh daddy!' She slapped him lightly on the shoulder.

August looked at Henry and smiled. "He's such a good daddy."

***

Beck came inside and threw his hat toward the nail. It was too late to take Lottie back over to the barn that night. Besides, he wasn't sure how to tell her he had paid a fortune teller to tell his future. She was one that believed that if what you have is a God-given ability, you'd never take pay for it. God's gifts were not for sale. But he'd have to tell her, especially if there was money they could get from that room.

Lottie picked up the hat and brushed off the mud. She carefully hung it up. One could tell what kind of day Beck had ever since he started wearing a hat. If he came in and hung it on the nail, he was in a fairly good humor. If he threw it at the nail, like he just did, he was upset about something. If he threw it in the floor and went back out on the porch, everybody needed to take cover and let the storm die down before they talked to him.

The next morning, Beck laid an extra axe into the bed of the truck. August stayed home this time, and Lottie and Norabell came to pile brush and rake away sawdust. Norabell's feller was to begin work today at the saw mill Beck had set up the day before. Jake had worked for the man that sold it to him, and he'd be a great help in running it. It would also be useful to have the motor running in the background to hide his chopping through the wall in the tack room.

They topped the hill after leaving August's house in the holler on Idaho Road. The smoke was billowing up from the direction where he was sure that Dugan Holler lay.

"Hold on," he said to Lottie and Norabell, "that looks like our place on fire. I hope its' not the woods burning. Surely it's too wet for them to catch fire."

When they got there, the neighbors had gathered. Everyone had a bucket in their hand. They stood and watched the barn finish burning to the ground. His barn. His barn with the secret room. The treasure was gone.

The constable for the area stood with the others.

"What happened?" Beck yelled.

The neighbor at the bottom of the hill on the main road slapped him on the back. "Bet it was lightning."

"There was rain, but I don't remember any thunder." Beck pulled off his hat and ran his fingers through his thin hair.

The constable stepped beside him. "I agree. Don't think it was lightning. I'd say somebody burned it for you. It's too wet to have caught fire on its own. Probably had to burn from the inside out."

One by one they came by and gave their condolences and offered to help him rebuild if he would call them when he had the lumber. Beck pieced together a story from various remarks made to him.

There were fresh footprints seen on the hill from the west side of Dugan Holler leading to his place, tracks both coming and going. It looked like they had made about three trips to and from the barn. Two sets of footprints. One large, most likely a man's. A smaller set, either a woman's or child's size.

Norabell and Lottie followed him around as he asked questions.

"I know what you're thinking, Daddy. They didn't do it. I don't care what you think. They would not burn the barn. Others think they're thieves and scoundrels, but PeNellie says it's not true. Not any more of them are crooks than there are crooks among our kind." Norabell swept her hand toward the crowd of people that stood around them as the last embers of the fire died away.

The constable reached out and shook Beck's hand. "I'm really sorry about this. Do you have any idea who might've burnt your barn?"

The sad face on Norabell made him want to not mention the ones he suspected, but somebody had purposely burned his property.

Beck laid his hand on Norabell's shoulder. "Penelope may not be a thief, but her grandmother told me about a room in this barn that nobody knew about."

"Are you talking about the gypsies at the head of the holler?" The constable asked.

Norabell screamed. "They're not gypsies. Don't call them that. They don't like it. They're Roma." She turned to Beck. "They didn't do it, I tell you."

Jake had helped fight the fire for as long as he could. He laid down on the bank of the creek, weak with exhaustion. He jumped up and ran when he heard Norabell scream. He stood behind her and put a hand on each of her shoulders. She jerked away.

"Norabell, Roma and gypsy are the same." He raised his voice as he tried to reason with her. "PeNellie's grandmother told me there was money in a room in the barn. They knew it was there. Of course, they would steal it."

Tears ran down Norabell's face. "What's wrong with all of you? That's the point. If they already knew there was money there, they would've taken it a long time ago if they had a mind to steal it. They wouldn't have waited until last night. In fact, they would have never told you about it. Somebody wants it to look like they did it."

Beck looked at the constable who agreed. "She has a point."

Jake walked Norabell to the truck. "Go home and get some rest. You're black from the smoke. I'll help your Daddy clear up as soon as it cools down a bit. There'll be others that will pitch in, too."

Norabell nodded.

"Norabell, your daddy is right. You need to stay away from those Gypsies. They're a bad lot. Never tell them what you have in your home. Anything you tell them might be something that makes them steal from you."

She stared at him and spoke with her teeth clenched tightly. "That's a hateful thing to say. You've never met them. You don't know anything about them. PeNellie is my friend, my only friend here. She'd never do anything like that, and I don't believe her Mamia would either."

Norabell slammed the door of the truck and turned away from him.

***

It was easy for some people to suspect a person of something, but it was not in Lottie's nature to do that. She slipped away from the others on the excuse of looking in the woods for ginseng. It wasn't a lie. On her walk to find the gypsies, she would make sure she found some, if there was any to be found.

Lottie took people at face value. What they were to her was what they would always be unless they proved different. She didn't plan on that changing because someone thought they knew something about them. Everyone felt the gypsies had burned the barn. Something inside her didn't believe them.

The older woman was outside stirring in a cast iron pot with a homemade paddle. Lottie coughed. "No need to give me a warning. I know you're back there. What do you want?"

"My name is Lottie, and I live down the holler from you."

"I also know who you are. We've already met. Did you come to ask me about the barn that burned?

"That is one reason. I wanted you to tell me what you think happened. Some think you did it. For some reason, I don't."

The woman turned and looked Lottie from head to toe. "You're wiser than the others. You're a kindred seer, as well."

Lottie smiled. "We may talk about that at some time. Right now, I need to know why someone would burn our barn."

She turned back to the pot and started to stir again. Finally she spoke. "I have no real knowledge of who did it. No matter what others say, or even what I may say at times, I don't know all things. It could be that someone overheard my talk with your husband." She stirred the pot. "I may have mentioned it to another. Not saying that I did, but it could be a possibility."

"I think you know if you did or not. Why would you mention it?" Lottie moved in front of the woman. Only the pot and the fire coals it sat upon was between them.

"Sometimes, I think that dropping the names of those that may have enlisted my help, and a dab of what was said, might make others believe." She looked up at Lottie.

"I don't blame you for the fire. I don't believe you set it. My purpose was to assure myself that you did not steal anything like others have suggested."

The woman raised her chin. "I don't steal. We are strangers. People are more apt to blame a stranger than their own." She looked deep into Lottie's eyes. "Or their neighbors." She took a long wooden dipper and poured some of the liquid she had stirred into the pan that she picked up from the ground. "Either way, it cannot be proven. Count your blessings it was your barn and not your house that they burned. My family in Germany had their house burned several times."

Lottie stood silent as the woman stirred the pot. When she looked up at her, Lottie said, "Where does your ability come from to see things in the future?"

"Where does yours?"

Lottie thought for a moment. "My Momma told me it's a gift from God. Somewhat like prophesy. I don't understand all I would like to about it. There are many things I don't get to know about before it happens. Some I do. It confuses me. There seems to be no reason for the ones that I do know. Not really. Many others, I would've like to have known before, then I could've changed them."

"Maybe that is why you didn't know. Perhaps it was for you to go through them, and grow from it."

"Some things I did know before they happened, I was not able to change. Why did I need to know, if I could do nothing about it?" Lottie moved away from the smoke that filled her face. She walked close to the older woman.

"That is one question I can't answer. It could be that you were less shocked, better able to accept those things. Maybe not. It's just a guess." She went back to stirring the pot.

"I'm very sorry that your family's house was burned. My family has had the same thing happened.   Homes   burned   for   reasons unknown to them."   She watched the silent woman rock back and forth as she stirred.

Lottie   smiled.   "My   child   and   your granddaughter will make great friends."   The woman looked up at the mention of the girls.

"They are much alike. Very inquisitive and desire to know things that sometimes will do them more harm than good. Nothing escapes them."   She watched Lottie closely.   "They search for knowledge where they think there are secrets.   Secrets are usually made for a reason. I, for one, think secrets are wrong. A person has to decide who they're protecting when they use secrets. It's never who it seems at first."   She walked to the porch and got a small jar. She spooned in a pale green liquid. "This is for you to take home.   It has that ginseng you were looking for as well as a few other herbs.   It's good for what ails you, no matter what that is." She laughed.

Lottie   took   the   jar.   "Thank   you   very much."

Chapter 6

Living In Dugan Holler

The early morning fog settled over the waters of the branch, and now the white mist rose high enough to hide the tallest of tree branches. It left the lower ones wet and dripping. As one looked up the hill, the fog again covered everything down to the ground spiraling up like smoke. It hid the world from the two that stepped out of their newly completed house.

Lottie and Beck took their cups of coffee and carefully walked across a log that spanned the branch. There were two stumps, side by side, that Beck had left during his tree cutting, both about knee high. They were perfect for a stool to sit on and listen to the babbling water. The gentle light of morning overcame the darkness and settled into the valley.

"Listen to that wind as it sings through the trees." Lottie leaned her head back and looked above her. "Sometimes I hear it saying something. It's never quite where I can make out the words, but I know it's talking."

The wind blew Lottie's hair into her face. Beck leaned over and pushed it behind her ear. "You have always been very mindful of nature and what happens around you. Although I don't know why it does, you still surprise me with what you see and know."

She smiled at him, then turned and looked at the house, still dark inside except for light from the fireplace in the kitchen.

"This is the most beautiful house I've ever laid eyes on."

Beck turned toward the house. "It's what I always wanted to build for you. Do you remember us talking about how we wanted a two story house? One that all the rooms in it was ours. Not like those houses in the mill towns at Clifton, South Carolina or the ones in Morganton, North Carolina."

Lottie smiled at him. "I even tried my hand at drawing it once. If I had a really good hand for sketching, it would have looked just like this one."

Beck reached into his back pocket and took out his leather billfold. He carefully took out a time-worn paper and unfolded it. It was the picture she had drawn. It was almost faded away from wear and tear.

"You kept it! Why would you do that?"

"Lottie, you've never asked for much in our marriage. I could probably count on one hand all the times you ever said 'I want' about any material thing. I swore to myself that if I could ever make it happen, you'd get this house. It was on my mind all those hot, hot days in the mill. It was renewed every time we lost a child and with every move we made. It was my wish when a star shot through the sky, when I saw the first star at night and said the childish saying of 'star light, star bright, first star I see tonight. I wish I may, I wish I might, have the wish that I wish tonight'. I even wished it when I blew out the candle on a cake you made for my birthday...the first birthday cake I ever had with a candle. You deserve this and more."

Lottie's face burned as he looked at her. "I don't deserve none of this. It's a blessing far beyond what I'm worthy of."

***

Saturday mornings had become a day unlike the ones in North Carolina. Every day there, but the Sabbath, had been for work. Finally, Norabell had one day of doing what she pleased, although her daddy had told her that would end when they were farmers and a crop had to be gotten out of the field. It could be a seven day work week until the harvest ended if the crops depended on it.

But for now, her daddy and Momma spent much of the day in town. Momma window shopped and walked the square area around the courthouse. Daddy sat in the corner and swapped stories with other men, whose wives were also window looking. The men would sit on a bench and whittle. The women would stop when they met someone they knew and gossip about the war. They promised to pray for each other's sons that had left for service.

Norabell had every intention of walking across the holler and over to Idaho to visit August. First she wanted to sit by the water and think about Jake. She really, really liked him. He seemed to feel the same, but Norabell kept hoping that he would mention marriage soon.

"It's a pretty day to sit and think." Norabell jumped.   Penelope Welch stood across the stream.

'I didn't hear you come up, Penelope."

The two girls smiled. Penelope pulled off her shoes and waded across. "You've known me long enough to now call me PeNellie like everyone else does, and you've proved and earned our friendship. The constable came by after your barn burned. He told us how you took up for the Roma."

"Alright. I liked the nickname PeNellie." Norabell pointed to the stump near her. "I knew that neither you nor your family could do such a thing. We found out that people tried to make the authorities believe it was you. They followed the tracks that they thought was from your place but found they circled back to the far part of our farm on the south side. Nowhere near you."

"I think we might be somewhat responsible. I think Mamia told someone about a secret room in a barn near where she lived. She did not name you, but they must have snooped until they found out. I'm very sorry."

"It's not a problem. The money, if it was really there, was never ours anyway. The barn is now rebuilt, and the house is complete. I love living in Dugan Holler."

PeNellie sat down. "There aren't many people that want to be friends with me. I thought we might visit occasionally...that is when I have a free day and so do you."

"Saturdays are good for me. I usually stay home while Momma and Daddy go to town. As soon as the dishes are washed from breakfast, the day is all mine to do as I wish."

"Ah! That's good." PeNellie bit her lip. "This is the second house we've lived in since coming to Lawrence County."

Norabell raised her eyebrows. "So you don't own where you live? Why did you leave the other house?"

PeNellie glanced at Norabell. "It had much to do with Mamia. She sometimes gets us into trouble."

"That sweet old woman? How could she ever cause trouble?"

"Much easier than you think! Her antics of telling fortunes before anyone asks her is one reason." She laughed.

"I thought it was fun. It's almost like a game to see if she's right about anything."

PeNellie folded her hands in her lap. "At least with you, she did not demand payment for her services even though you didn't ask for a reading. My Papa has forbidden her to tell fortunes here again, but she does not listen well. I know she does it, but I don't feel right tattling on her. She is my elder."

"Since she's not charging, surely your Papa wouldn't care."

"She doesn't charge for the first one, but the second and third...that's another story. The first is to get their attention. For some reason, she did extract payment from your daddy, though."

Norabell turned toward her friend. "Does she know all things that will happen? She was sure right about that room, so my daddy said."

"Of course, she doesn't know everything. If she did, surely she would be more careful than to get us kicked out of every house we move into." PeNellie laughed. "Our people are not liked well anywhere we go. There are things that they say about us that aren't true. Some things are true, I guess, but they don't understand our history. And they don't want to listen if we try to tell them."

"I'll listen."

PeNellie began, "I hadn't planned on talking about this with you. But, let me say that I don't tell fortunes, kidnap children, or steal. There are people in our clan that have stolen. That's why our family pulled away from the group.   There are other reasons, too. Across the sea, with this war, Hitler is killing the Roma. We have family and friends that have died. Word has come to us that if people know we are Roma, they might put us in camps like they have in Germany.   Please don't tell anyone about Mamia telling your fortune or your daddy's." She frowned. "It's probably necessary this time that I tell Papa what she's done."

Norabell swallowed hard. "I'm sorry about your family in Germany.

PeNellie put her hand over Norabell's. "Thank you so much. I believe you mean that. I'm sure people mean no hard feelings in calling us Gypsy, but we prefer to be called Roma. I don't know how you knew that when you told the constable we were Roma."

"I heard you tell that the first time I met you. I went to the library in town and looked it up. I wanted to know more."

"See...you're a good friend.   You don't judge until you know. And for the record, we don't move around because we like to travel. People are mean to us in most places we go. Many have already tried to settle down, but this war has most of us on the move again."

"I won't tell anyone about you, even if they ask. We're friends, and I won't let them hurt you."

PeNellie squeezed her hand. "If we stay that long. I do hear words from my Papa that sound like he is ready to move on. I hope not. Not when I found a real friend. My first ever." She waded into the water, but stopped mid-stream and looked back. "About that room. Mamia studies people. And the land. She follows other people's footprints to see where they will lead her. You can learn a lot that way, she tells me. There is very little that gets by her observant eyes." She walked to the other side and returned from where she had come.

***

Jake and Norabell rode home in the wagon from church with Will Carver and his wife. It appeared strange to her that she would have friends her age that were already married. Will and his wife had gotten hitched last September. Behind them in another wagon was Will's dad, Punch Carver and his wife. Will's Momma had fixed lunch and invited them to their house.

"Uh oh." There were feathers strewn across the yard. "Dad is not going to be happy.

That's his best chickens." The bodies were nowhere to be seen, but there were sure a lot of feathers.

Punch pulled up beside them. He looked at the yard and turned pale. In one leap, he was off the wagon and headed toward their neighbor's house.

Dawson heard Punch yelling long before he got to the edge of road between their farms. The young couples had followed at a safe distance and could hear every word.

"Get out here Dawson. Where is that egg-sucking dog of yours?" Punch walked closer to the house and yelled again.

"Hold your tater, Carver. The dog was asleep on the back porch." Dawson turned and yelled at the dog that came around the house at a trot. "Come on Buck. Here, here." The dog came and sat down at his feet. He growled when Punch took another step.

Punch gritted his teeth. "He's been in my chickens. I came home to find feathers all over the yard. They were my best layers. It was the Dominicker hens.

Dawson squatted down and rubbed Buck from head to toe, looking in his mouth, under this chin, and down his neck. "It wasn't my dog. He don't have a feather anywhere on

him. There's no blood on his body anywhere.
Maybe it was your own dog."

Punch spat on the ground at his side. "I've
had my dog for five years. He's never touched
a chicken. Don't think he would start now. It
has to be yours."

Dawson stood up and looked to the west
and then turned his head toward the north.
"There are three other houses with their
chimneys in sight of your house. It might be
one of theirs. Could even be a stray. Maybe a
fox. I just know for sure, it wasn't mine."

"You might have already washed him up in
the creek by now. There were feathers on the
ground in this direction. It had to be your dog.
I expect pay for those hens."

Dawson shook his head. "You're not
getting a penny from me. I'm not going to pay
for something my dog didn't do in order to
keep you happy. Look further on down the
road, Punch Carver. Get that chip off your
shoulder and move on. While you're here, I
saw you putting up some barb wire on both
sides of the road near your house. You better
not ever put it across that road, or you'll wish
you hadn't."

Punch kept walking like he didn't hear.

Jake and Norabell waited until the others
went around back to go into the house.

"I don't like this fighting. Can we go home?" She twisted the handkerchief in her hand.

"They done fixed food for us. We might find a way to leave after that. It would be bad manners to not eat. As soon as the meal is over, it might be fine. Us and Will and his wife can all go down to the water and play in the creek after dinner. Don't worry. It'll all blow over. They fight all the time."

Norabell's legs felt like mush. Jake took her arm and led her around to the back of the house. Punch jerked open the back door and stepped back into the kitchen. Behind him was his wife with a broom. A bird flew out of the house and swooped over Norabell's head.

Although at the time, she had felt that she would never remember, the gypsy's word echoed in her head. *For where the bird doth fly, the man will die, in anger he hath left in gall, there his spirit again may call.*

She shivered.

Chapter 7

August and Norabell sat side by side on the steps.

Lottie sat in the swing. She laid the shirt she had been repairing on her knee. The last light of day was dimming, and shadows of trees fell across the porch. The fading light had put a strain on her eyes as she sewed. The light faded into a million shades of red beyond the massive trees of the western border of Dugan Holler.

Lottie leaned toward Beck and said, "I love to sit on the porch on a cool September night and listen to the crickets and frogs croaking down by the creek. It's so peaceful. Thank you for making this swing for my front porch, Beck. This is my favorite place to be in the late afternoon."

"Norabell, go around to the side porch and get you girls a chair. They're just around the corner." Beck said as he looked up from the Democrat Union he'd been reading.

August smiled. "We're just fine daddy. I like sitting on the steps with my little sister." She twirled Norabell's hair around her finger.

Lottie smiled and shook her head at the two of them sitting there talking about their week. "Friday nights have turned into a real family night in Dugan Holler. I think we should make this a weekly event."

"Do I get included on this family gathering?" Jake said from the side of the house.

Everyone laughed. Norabell ran to him and gave him a hug.

"Glad to have you, young man. You did a lot of hard work today, and you deserve a rest." Beck went to the other side of the house and brought around a couple of chairs.

August rose and sat in the chair. "You can sit by Norabell on the steps. I'll sit here with Momma and Daddy."

Jake was still red from Norabell's hug that she had given him in front of the others. He looked at Norabell. "I wanted to ask Norabell," He looked up at her parents, "and both of you too, if I can take her to a street dance in Lawrenceburg tomorrow night. My brother and his wife are going, and he said we could ride with them. He's a good driver. I can have her home by 11:00."

Lottie looked at Beck, who then turned to the young man. "I'm not much on dancing. I tend to agree with the preacher that it's the devil's work."

"Ah Daddy. Would it be wrong to watch the others dance? We don't have to dance do we, Jake?"

Jake shook his head. "Of course not, if you don't want her to."

Beck looked back at the paper. "I see they have a write up about it here in the DU. It's their first street dance ever in Lawrence County."

"They're going to hang the canvas sidewall which they once used to circle the football field at the school. It'll cover 400 feet of West Gaines from North Military all the way to Mahr Avenue. This is going to be an annual event from now on for the Poultry Festival," Jake explained.

Beck looked up from the paper. "Boy, you quoted that almost exact. You must have read it quite a few times."

The others laughed.

"I wanted to get everything right so I could explain it to you when I asked if she could go. I didn't know you got the DU."

Norabell raised her shoulders up and squeezed her fists in front of her chin waiting for his answer.

Jake explained to Lottie. "The music is going to be by a group out of Memphis, Tennessee. His name is Hal Burns. He's bringing his orchestra. It'll be worth the trip just to listen to some big band music. I've heard them on the radio." He looked back to Norabell. "We can see them playing live...better than the Victrola or the radio." He looked back to her parents

They laughed.

"I'm going to let her go. Only because it's you, and I know you'll take good care of her. Because you know if you don't, you don't have a job. You also know I own a gun. "

Jake turned red.

"Oh Daddy. Quit teasing him." Norabell stood up and took Jake's arm. "Let's take a walk. The moonlight coming through the trees down by the water is so pretty at night." She turned to Beck and stuck out her tongue playfully. "We'll still be in sight, Daddy."

They walked down to the creek and sat down on one of the stumps with their backs leaning against each other and talked. Some things were easier talked about when you didn't have to look each other in the eye.

* * *

"So you'd read all about that dance already, had you?" Lottie said to Beck.

"I read pretty much everything in the paper when I buy it. I want to be sure I get my money's worth."

August laughed at them. "I'm heading home. Henry should be back by now. He's been in town making plans for us to have a cotton crop next year. He met with a group of men to talk about buying their seed together to get a better price. We got some of the land cleared and ready. Hopefully, someday we can build a house as nice as yours on our farm. See you Sunday at Church."

Lottie went inside. She brought a kerosene lamp and sat it on a table. Beck drug a chair up beside it and pulled the paper close to the light.

He looked up. "My plan for the rest of the fall and winter is to clear the land in the lower holler where I did some clear cutting. We can dig up the stumps and burn off the land. I'll turn it up and let it sit most of the winter. I want to do a patch of cotton. I've been talking to the men on the square about it, and reading the paper and anything else I can get my hands on. It can bring us quite a chunk of money. I'll talk to Henry about getting in on buying the seed in bulk. We're pretty much out of money from our savings and selling your part of your Papa's land. It's time to make this farm pay for itself. I don't want to cut any more of the timber. It's still growing thick with large trees all the way to Nubbin Ridge Road and on the west side. Buying the lumber mill helped us get this house built and make the payments at the bank until now. It's time to find other ways to make money. I'll try to sell the saw mill. The bank expects the payment no matter what. My word is my bond, and I'll pay this off, no matter what it takes."

"I thought the same thing about the cotton planting. I'll try to be a little tighter with what money we do have. We need to have our own garden next year and not depend on August's land for that. They can reduce the size of their garden and have more cotton. They say cotton is a family crop. It takes everyone working."

"We're old, but I think we still have a few crops in us. I'd rather die in the field as on a death bed." Beck declared. "We'll make money as best we can in these bad times."

"As luck would have it, somebody came by to rent the smaller of the older houses today. A young couple. She's going to have a baby before long. He works for the Harpers on their farm. Right now, they live with her parents in town. He needs to move to be closer to his work." Lottie clapped her hands.

"Good. That'll help." Beck nodded and went back to the paper. "What's their name? Did you get any money?"

"I did. The money is in the sugar bowl. The couple is Weston and Connie Caudill."

***

The street dance in Lawrenceburg made Norabell feel like she was living in the cotton mill towns again. People came from everywhere. Jake parked his brother's automobile some distance from the area. There was a designated area for automobiles and a separate place for wagons.

"I never thought I'd live anywhere there would be more cars and trucks than wagons." Norabell said as they walked toward the crowd of people.

Jake put his arm around her and pulled her through the crowd to where they could see the band play.

She watched his foot tap to the beat of the music. "We can dance. Daddy will never know, if we don't tell him."

"He might not know, but I would. If I tell a fellow something, he can count on my word. What kind of person would I be, if he couldn't count on me to be honest?"

Norabell smiled. This was another thing that made her love him. LOVE. She had known from the time they started writing that he was the 'one', but this sealed it for her. She had seen lots of people back in the mill towns that weren't always true to their words. Especially young men.

Jake took her elbow. "Let's walk around and see if there are any people we know."

It was too crowded near the band, so they pulled to the back of the crowd and used another street to walk to the outer edges of the group further down the street.

"Look. There's Punch Carver. I wonder if his family is with him. Let's say hello."

Before they could wave, Norabell saw Punch's face turn red as he stared in front of him. One glance in the direction he was staring told the story. Dawson was talking to Mrs. Carver. They were laughing. Jake didn't see it and pulled her along toward them.

"Jake. Let's not get so close. I don't think this is going to be a pretty sight. Look where he's heading." They stopped within hearing distance.

Punch grabbed his wife by the arm and jerked her around.

"Hey, don't be so rough, Punch. She's not a plow horse."

Punch pulled her behind him. "She's anything I want her to be. She's MY wife. Don't you have a wife of your own?"

"I do. She went with the others down to see the band play."

Punch's wife pulled on his arm. "I was just saying hello to our neighbors. We can go now. Let's not cause any trouble."

He jerked her hand from his arm. "No trouble is going on. Just wanted to say my hello's to the neighbors, too."

"You've said them. Let's go."

"You go stand over…" Punch saw us. "Go over there with Jake and Norabell. I'll be right along."

Norabell crooked her finger for Mrs. Carver to come to them. All the way, the older woman wrung her hands and kept glancing over her shoulder.

"He'll come in a minute, Mrs. Carver. We'll stay with you until he does."

She shook her head hard. "He's got a hot temper. Anything can set it off. I'm scared he'll do something bad."

Wide-eyed, Norabell looked at her. "Like what?"

One look at the young girl, and the woman took a deep breath. "Oh, it's just me and my nervousness. Everything will be fine." She turned back to the men and yelled. "Come on, Punch. It's too crowded. Let's get on home."

Their words were so quiet that the others could not hear, but the scowl on their faces made Norabell know, it was not a pleasant, neighborly conversation. Shortly, Punch came toward them.

He came up and took his wife's elbow. A man that Norabell remembered seeing at church stopped in front of them. "What are you going to do about him, Punch?"

Punch spat in the direction of Dawson. "I guess I'll have to kill him before this is over."

They all stared at Punch.

"Let's go Punch," his wife said.

"What's going on with Dawson?" Jake asked.

"Nothing I can't handle. He looks harmless enough, but looks can be deceiving. I've known him some time, and he knows what makes me angry. Those are the things he tries to do. I shouldn't let him get to me, but I can't help it."

Norabell thought he looked ashamed of his actions. She felt better about the situation.

They left, and the young couple made a circle of the people, speaking to friends of Jake's. There were even a few from the church.

Jake put his arm around her and pointed to three young men standing at the back of the crowd. "See those boys?"

She nodded.

"They just joined the army. They told me last night."

Norabell stared at them. "They're not old enough to go to war."

"Two of them are sixteen. They lied about their age. The other is seventeen. His parents told him to lie about his age, and they would vouch for him if anybody asked. He's given them a lot of trouble the past two years. They think the army will do him good."

Norabell was horrified. "What do you mean that it will do him good? It could get him killed."

"He could end up in prison if he stays here. The sheriff came looking for him last week."

They watched girls come up and talk to the boys.

"I'm ready to go home, if you are." Norabell said.

Jake looked surprised. "Sure. If that's what you want."

Norabell shook her head, and they left.

***

The Caudill couple had only been living in the house a week when Lottie saw the man ride as hard as he could toward the house astride a big black stallion. He never slowed as he passed Lottie and Norabell standing on the porch.

Lottie looked at Norabell. "Guess the baby is a-coming. I'll go down and see if they need any help. Do you want to come?"

Norabell took a step back. "I don't think so. The first baby I see come into this world should be my own. You go right ahead. I'm pretty sure I'll have these jars washed by the time you get back."

In about twenty minutes, Norabell heard her mother laughing as she came toward the house. Lottie sat down on the front steps.

"What's wrong?   Has the baby already come? That was about as quick as I ever heard of a woman having a baby."

Lottie's breath came in gulps between her laughter and trying to catch her breath from the walk. "I can't wait to tell your Daddy this one. I felt plumb sorry for the husband."

"Tell me what happened."

"I will, but you have to promise that I get to tell the story to your daddy."

Norabell nodded.

"The young man was working on the Harper farm. Before he left this morning, he told his little city wife that if she needed anything...meaning if she was about to have the baby, I'm sure...that she was to send word to him and he'd come straight home. That friend of yours, PeNellie, passed by about two hours ago. She was headed to the Harpers to help in the garden. Connie Caudill told her to tell Weston to come back right now. She told him. He borrowed a horse and rode like the wind to get here." Lottie started to laugh so hard she got the hiccups.

"As I ran toward their house, I could see him slide right off that horse and run through the front door. Never even tied it up. By the time I arrived, she was standing over him, fanning him with a funeral home fan. When he had come through the door like lightning out of the sky, she was sitting there shelling peas. She told him she was lonely and wanted him to come home and keep her company."

Norabell's eyes widened, and she began to sputter. "LONELY!!!! Oh my! I bet he was madder than a hornet. I think we should save this for our next Friday night family get together and tell everyone."

Chapter 8

September 1942

People worked hard for a living. None felt poorer than the others as each one struggled to feed their families and keep up the payments on their farms. There were more conveniences than ever before, but many could either not afford them, or they were rationed for the war effort. Each season brought hardships and its own set of trials.

Spring in Tennessee showed up with buttercups and crocus, often shooting out between patches of a late snow. Spring rains created a 'fresh"…a small flood that cleaned out the creek beds. It filled up old swimming holes and washed out new ones. Neighbors gathered to clear the banks of trash and to pull gravel back into deep holes in the ford of the creek that could easily stall a wagon or automobile.

As for the new places to swim…it didn't take the young people long to find them. The local favorite was below Dugan Holler just as you crossed Sugar Creek on the way to Punch's house. It became the place for the farmer's children to swim, courting couples to hide away for some private time, and family's to gather for Sunday afternoon picnics. They took lunch to eat and pulled their car or truck to the middle of the stream and washed them. The dirt roads often left thick dust settled on the automobiles. It was important for them to have a clean car for Sunday church. As they had washed them on late Saturday afternoon, the family would drive slowly to church Sunday morning in order to keep from getting them as dusty. The churches did their part in keeping up morale on the home front. There were box suppers and candy pulls. Spring revivals and summer camp meetings spoke to the spirit and soul. Sons going away to war caused the churches to be fuller than usual. They prayed for one another's children and inquired about letters from the front lines of the war.

Fall brought the County Fair and the Poultry Festival, cotton picking was pushed in full swing. School let out for two weeks to help the family gather the crops. One day, during the fair, they let the school children in free.

The war that year on the home front had heated up considerably, and rationing had been implemented for many things including tires, cars, gas, and sugar. Beck's and Lottie's first crop of cotton had been a bumper one as had August's and Henry's. In spite of it, there were things you couldn't buy. Even if it wasn't rationed, some wares did not get to the stores because of the gas and tire regulations

A plan was made for Beck, Lottie, and Norabell as well as August and her family, and a few friends from church, to meet at August's and Henry's house on Saturday afternoon, September 20, 1942. Henry had come home with a great surprise for August's birthday. He had been saving for months and had ordered it last spring. It had come just in time last week for him to give it to her. A new Zenith table radio with push-button tuning.

They climbed into the truck and headed off to August's and Henry's. The war was boiling hot on the front lines. Like many others during that year, they planned to gather to discuss the fighting. The older people were going to listen to the news on the new radio. Norabell had talked her sister into a promise to let the young people listen to some music in between news broadcasts.

Norabell scooted to the edge of the seat and put her arms on the dashboard. "Momma, I don't like listening to the news about the war. There's too much death. At church, somebody told some of them about a telegram that came to the lady that sits on the pew beside them announcing that her son has died. Then others started talking about a friend or the brother of their best friend that had either died or lost a leg or arm. I don't even like to look at the newspaper."

Lottie nodded. "I noticed she wasn't there Sunday and asked about her welfare. Someone told me she had taken to her bed. I got a letter this week that three boys from Morganton died in a battle. They were cousins. You have to understand that these are the same reasons I DO want to listen. I need to know who has lost their loved ones. They're people that I know. Losing a limb in the war at least means they may come home alive."

"Why is our country fighting over there? I don't understand why people have to fight anyway. Can't we all get along and live our own lives?"

"We were first fighting for people's freedom in other countries. Then they bombed Pearl Harbor last year." Lottie stopped and opened her purse. She laid her handkerchief to the side. The paper she pulled was wrinkled, and she smoothed it on her knee. "I cut this out of a paper a few months ago, and I carry it with me. It says it best. It said some things that I like..." She had underlined a few lines from a story.

> "...I shall always remember someone, it may have been Theodore Roosevelt saying, in my hearing when I was young, that when you were afraid to do a thing, that was the time to go and do it. Every time we shirk making up our minds or standing up for a cause in which we believe, we weaken our character and our ability to be fearless...[i]

"Our country has to stand up for what we believe in just like each of us do every day that we live." Lottie told Norabell.

Norabell frowned. "It would be one thing if they went over there and defended what we believe and then came back. They're not coming back!"

Beck said, "It makes me feel guilty that I'm too old to help defend our country and the things we believe in."

Lottie's voice rose. "I'm glad you're too old, as are my sons. But I have grandsons and other family that might have to go. We need to pray for our nation to win this nasty war." She turned to Norabell. "What about Jake? Will he be going off to war?"

"I hope not. I don't think I could stand being without him. We just got to know each other. But he warned me that if something doesn't happen, his number may come up. I know he's no better than the others that are having to go, but I'm praying he gets to stay here. His older brother left last week. He's the only son left to take care of his Momma and daddy."

"Do you think the fighting will come over here? People at church were talking about building bomb shelters."

Beck gripped the steering wheel. "It is a possibility. Our government is preparing for it, I know. The newspaper said they're having a county-wide blackout this coming week on Thursday."

"What does that mean?" Lottie asked.

"All power is to be shut down all over the county. No glows of any kind. If you have to have lights, then you are to cover your windows with dark material. Not even lights from cars. Nothing."

"We don't have electricity. We don't have to worry. We'll stay home." Lottie said.

"Not even kerosene lights are to be burning. Complete darkness. It's a drill in case the enemy's airplanes fly over here with bombs like they did Pearl Harbor. They'll never know that there are people here and pass on by. It will look like fields with no sign of life."

"I'm scared." Norabell leaned closer to her Daddy.

Everyone was quiet until Lottie spoke. "Who all is coming to August's from the church young people?"

Norabell was happy they weren't talking about the war anymore. "There'll be Jake, Will Carver, and Will's wife. There will also be Will's cousin from New York. I think her name is Katherine. They moved to Nashville from New York when her daddy lost all his money a few years ago. Jake said times are still hard for them, and they moved to Lawrence County where it's more rural, he said. They need to grow their own food and, hopefully one day, buy a farm and raise cotton. They're dreamers, Jake said. I've not met her yet."

"I'm glad that you'll have friends there."

Norabell linked arms with Lottie. "I would've been just fine if it was only Jake and myself. But it still should be fun."

"There's safety in numbers. With the others there, I can let them chaperone you while we have a good time." Lottie patted her child's arm.

"Oh, Momma. I'm not a child anymore, and Jake is a perfect gentleman."

"I'm happy to hear that."

Norabell patted her feet like she was running on the floor of the truck. "Hurry Daddy. We're going to be late."

"Hush, girl. I'm not going to overheat the engine of this truck. It has to last a long time. We're almost there."

**

The others had already arrived and were sitting on the porch and in the yard. Some had brought straight chairs and others old quilts which they spread on the ground. The radio was loud and music could be heard long before they got out of the truck.

August reached inside the door and pulled out a couple of straight chairs. "Momma and Papa, sit here on the porch. Norabell, sit over on the quilt further out in the yard. Some of the younger group brought it for all of you. Jake and Will walked to his cousin's house to get her Victrola and records."

Will's wife motioned for Norabell to sit on the quilt beside her. She whispered in her ear. "I have news. I'll tell you about it later.

Henry whooped loud. "That's Sons of the Pioneers singing Tumbling Tumbleweeds. August and I have listened to that a lot the last few days. Makes you feel like you're right there on the prairie out west."

The song was almost over when there was a static sound and a voice that said, "We interrupt this program to bring you a special report...." Then, there was the sound of a telegram coming in and the man began to read.

> *"We are getting news today that happened earlier in the week. It was kept top secret and released today. On September 15, the US aircraft carrier Wasp was torpedoed at Guadalcanal. On the 16th, there was a Japanese attack repelled on Port Moresby."*

He ended and told them stay tuned shortly for more news of the war.

Henry pulled out a board with a war zone map nailed to it. He had gotten it at the Esso service station in Lawrenceburg. The men walked over and discussed the foreign cities where the action had been named in the weeks before.

All of them gathered their chairs closer to the porch even though you could hear the radio just fine from the yard. They didn't want to miss a word.

"Momma..." Norabell hollered.   Lottie stood and waved a hand at her. She made a shushing noise and sat back down.

Norabell turned to the sound of voices coming across the yard. Five adults turned and shushed them also. Jake had a beautiful Victrola in his arms. Will's and the girl's arms were full of records.

They sat everything down, and Will introduced his cousin. "This is my cousin, Katherine. She just moved here. She thought we might enjoy some music while the others are listening to war news."

Katherine sat down beside Jake. "I thought it would be a good time while I had these strong men to help me bring all this down here and take it back."   She reached over and squeezed Jake's arm just above his elbow. He turned red, and she laughed and laid her head over on his shoulder.

"I'm proud of our service men. I think I'll listen to the war news." Norabell stood. "It's the least we can do to support them. We can listen to the music after the news goes off."

They looked at each other. Jake stood. "I'll go with you." He looked back apologetically. "There will be plenty of time for music and dancing. I think the war news only lasts fifteen minutes."

Norabell stared at him.

"I'm going with her." He turned and led Norabell to the porch. They sat on the bottom steps. The others slowly came over.

On September 19, 1942, two carriers, the Wasp and Battleship North Caroline, and ten other battle warships, were escorting the transport ships as they carried the 7Th Marine Regiment to Guadalcanal as reinforcements. The Wasp was drawn as the ready-duty carrier. Early in the morning, about an hour before sunrise, the Wasp was fueling planes and sent out the morning search plane. All was cleared with no contact with the Japanese during the *day, with the exception of a four-engine Japanese flying boat which they downed at 12:15.*

At 14:20, the carrier completed the recovery of 11 planes, then turned starboard, and heeled slightly as the course was changed. At 14:44 a lookout reported 'three torpedoes" three points forward of the starboard beam. All-in-all, a spread of six torpedoes were fired at the Wasp from the tubes of B1-type Submarine. Three struck the Wash in rapid succession, one broached and left the water and struck the ship slightly above the waterline. All hit near the gasoline tanks and magazines. Two passed ahead of the Wasp and passed two other ships, one hit while maneuvering to avoid the other torpedo. The sixth torpedo did not hit a ship but narrowly missed the Lansdown.

There were several explosions in the forward part of the ship with aircraft thrown about and fell to the deck with such force the landing gears were snapped. Other planes fell on the deck. Fire broke out all over the hangar and below decks, so heated that the ammunition for the anti-aircraft guns were detonated, and fragments sprayed the forward part of the ship.

Water remains in the forward part of the ship, and that part is inoperable. There is no water to squelch the fires and ammunition continued to be set off. Gasoline and oil was released from the tanks and began to burn on the water.

The captain commanded the boat be turned in order to change the position of the wind and keep the fire forward. After that all communication circuits died.

Before the ceasing of communication, there seemed to be no panic. More reports will become available as other ships in the area transfer the news.

This is your war report for September 19, 1942.

Jake asked, "Does anyone know if any men from Tennessee were stationed on the Wasp?"
The others turned and said together, "Shhh."
Jake walked back and sat on the quilt.
There was a sound of tapping like a telegram was coming through.

"We interrupt this for this announcement: Tomorrow will be the launching for the SS Patrick Henry...the first of what is planned to be many more Liberty ships. We will try to keep you informed on the success of this ship and the others to follow in this war.

Remember to support our troops. Listen in three times a day for the war report."

Beck and Lottie joined in the conversation of the group that was telling about how awful Hitler was. The rest of the younger people moved back to the quilt beside Jake.

Katherine leaned toward Jake and smiled. "I think I'll join the war. They're letting women fly bombers."

"I can't see you inside an airplane, much less flying one. You're a scaredy cat at heart," Will said.

Norabell leaned over and put her arm on Jake's. "I don't even like to talk about the war. It's sad that our boys are being killed. They're drafting more and more men every day."

"You don't support the war?" Katherine challenged her.

"I do support our boys, and the war. We have to fight for what we believe in. But I'm saying that it's sad, and I don't want our men to die over there. Who knows how long it will last?"

"I write to a dozen soldiers every week. The president has encouraged us to do that. It's important to keep up their morale. Everybody needs to do their part. There is much we can do, you know. Grow our own food so the farmers can send more to the soldiers. My mother made me a dress last week, and we noticed that the makers of patterns have changed so they don't use but half the material that they did before. Isn't that dandy? I know in reason that you all want to help, too. That is if you care about the soldiers like you say you do." She stared straight at Norabell who turned her head away from Katherine.

Jake put his arm around Norabell. "We'll win this war. The United States is the strongest nation there is. Now that we've joined in, it'll be over quick."

"I hope." Norabell took a deep breath and sighed. "I hope the fighting never comes over here. It could, you know. Daddy said so. They went to Pearl Harbor, and nobody thought they would do that."

Katherine pulled the Victrola toward her and opened the lid. "Let's listen to some music. Get us out of the mully-grubs. What song should I play?" She picked up the records and began to read off the titles. "These are all big band sounds. What about Aint She Sweet?" She glanced at the others. They started at her. "I also have…Don't Get Around Much Anymore, Seven Come Eleven, Googie Woogie Maxixe, Day In-Day Out." Nobody spoke. "I guess I'll have to choose." She flipped through more records. She looked up and smiled. "Artie Shaw and 'Oh Lady, Be Good"

Norabell had never danced in her life, but Will and Jake taught her some dance moves. It was fun. As much as she hated to admit it, Katherine was as good a dancer as her cousin Will. She just didn't like it when she pulled Jake up to dance with her.

The women brought out food and set it on a table in the yard. While they ate at the end of the afternoon, the sun slipped over the trees and out of sight. Henry turned the radio on again for them to listen to the Don Ameche show.

"Here she is folks. Miss Rita Hayworth. The prettiest woman to ever grace our microphone. You're looking good, Rita. That dress is stunning. *'What this old thing. I just threw it on.'* Must have been a curve."

The others laughed along with the radio.

Folks, we're going to hear that song from the movie Gila called 'Put The Blame on Mame."

Henry said, "I hear tell she mouth pantomimes that song. It's not even her voice. Not that I ever saw the movie."

He had become quite a resource for radio personalities since he had ordered the radio earlier in the year, even though August didn't understand why he cared about such things.

Next, we have Amos and Andy performing "Who's on First".

Every adult around stopped what they were doing and gathered close.

Henry talked loudly. "I hope Kingfish is on this one." He looked at the others. "I can't hardly wait until we have electricity out in these parts. Maybe we can get a television. Amos and Andy is on television now."

Will's wife leaned over and whispered in Norabell's ear. She put both of her hands over her mouth and jumped up and down. Then she reached out and hugged her friend.

Jake pulled Norabell over to the adults. She waved at the others and grabbed Jake's arm as he pulled her along. They listened to the show, laughing right along with the others.

For a little while, they forgot about men and women across the sea dying for freedom and about the hardships of life during World War II. It was a welcome relief.

***

Norabell waited for Jake and Will to take the things back to Katherine's house. Lottie and Beck helped August set the chairs in the house and put things away. Jake had told her when he got back with Will, he would take her home. Beck had agreed they could ride in the back of the truck, and Jake could walk home from there, if he wanted to go with them. She loved her daddy!

The ride home in the dark with the stars twinkling above them would have been quite romantic if Norabell was not still quite so irritated about Katherine. The girl had made it obvious she wanted to use Jake for a little distraction from the war talk.

"You know she's just playing with your feelings?" Norabell said aloud.

"Who?"

Norabell rolled her eyes. Although Jake could not see it, her silence said plenty.

"If you're talking about Katherine, she's not my type at all.   Besides, she don't really like me. Do you think I'm as dumb as I look?"

Norabell   laughed   and   pushed   him backward.   "You're so funny.   You seemed really taken with that girl the whole night. She even had you dancing with her, leaving me all alone."

Their feet hung over the tailgate of the truck, Norabell wrapped her leg around Jake's. She lightly hit his shoulder with her own. He leaned against her. She raised her other foot and kicked him playfully. Each one tried to get the last hit.

"We have a Victrola too, you know. Well, it's a Grafonola. Daddy bought it years ago for Momma."

"Oh really? I didn't know that." His laugh mixed with his words.

"Of course we only have four records, and they didn't play any of them tonight."

Jake laughed and took her hand. "I think somebody is a little jealous. Does that mean you like me more than you let on?"

"Hmph. I let on to you how much I like you. Plenty. You should have no question of how much I care.   There's not a person breathing that sees us together that wouldn't know that."

He pushed his shoulder tight against hers again and looked at the road behind them. 'Enough to marry me?"

Norabell leaned forward and looked at his face in the moonlight. "Don't you go teasing me, Jake Mince."

"There's nobody in the back of this truck teasing. At least not me. Will you marry me or not?"

She let out a whoop worthy of an Indian on the warpath. "Yes, I will."

Beck slowed down, stuck his head out the window, and yelled, "Everything all right back there?"

Jake yelled back. "Everything is fine and dandy. It was just Norabell acting silly."

Beck rolled his window up.

"You think I'm being silly? Or was that just for their benefit?"

Jake reached his arm around her and pulled her close. "All for their benefit. You just made me the happiest man alive. I want to yell as loud as you did to the whole world." He leaned back his head and opened his mouth…

"No…don't. Let's not say a word yet. I want to let it sink in to me first. Let's do some talking and planning together, then we'll tell the others. Does that seem agreeable? It's not like I'm gonna change my mind. I just want to feel like it's real and be excited with our secret. I love secrets!"

"Anything you want, my Norabell, my brown-eyed, red haired beauty."

He grunted when she pushed her elbow into this side.

"Hush now…I ain't no beauty. But as long as I have you fooled, I'm as happy as a lark."

Jake turned and looked through the back window of the truck to make sure no one was watching, then turned to kiss her on the cheek. Norabell turned at the same time, and their lips met. It was a quick kiss. They had kissed before, but not where others might have seen them. And this was the first time as his fiancé.

Chapter 9

The knowledge that she was getting married finally felt real to her. She was ready to share it with the rest of the world. The Friday night family get together would be the perfect time. August and Henry would be there. That part of the week had become her favorite time.

She was on the porch when her Daddy came in from work. "Where's Jake? I thought he might come by here on his way home like he generally does."

Beck sat down on the steps and took off his work boots. "He didn't work with me today. His Dad wanted him to help at their house. I can't complain. They've let him work with me for some time now without saying a word." He stretched out his legs and lay backward on the cool porch. "I think they must approve of the girl he's been going steady with for the past year. You didn't make them mad did you? I still need his help. I figure I pay as much as the next feller."

Norabell frowned. "They didn't act mad when I was there last. They were friendly at church Sunday. Do you think I really did something to make them not like me?"

Lottie walked out of the house. "Quit teasing her, Daddy. She believes every word you say." She patted her on the head. "His family told me Sunday that on Friday they needed Jake to go with his Papa to town. They were going to the livestock sale and get some hogs to fatten up until killing time. There's all kind of indications this might be a cold winter, and they can cure meat. They're trying to help their married son and daughter-in-law. She's expecting. Their other son is in the war and they are helping them, too."

Norabell looked up at her mother. "I know about the baby. She told me before she told anyone else. Other than her husband, I guess."

Lottie shook her head. "Come on in, and let's eat some supper. August will be over later."

"I hope Jake comes tonight."

The wind blew through the trees with a hard puff. Lottie walked to the edge of the porch and looked toward the west. "There's clouds rising up. I expect a rain to start after a bit. Not that I'm complaining. Listening to that rain hitting the roof makes me feel safe and dry in my wonderful home. But it might be too bad of weather for Jake to get out in it."

"I don't think weather would stop him. Not if he really, really cares about me." Norabell went in and slammed the door.

***

Beck yelled, "Where are you, Lottie?" He stepped out onto the porch where she sat in the swing, her eyes watching the rushing water from the eaves.

"Where am I? I guess I'm on the porch in Clifton, South Carolina. Listening to the rising water rush down the river. I can almost hear the screams and cries."

"Come on back to Dugan Holler. The water is not near that high and most likely never will be. It's not a good place to be going to in your mind. It's always better to look forward than to look back." Beck sat down beside her.

"I know. It's not like I meant to go there. It was the rain. Then the thought of August coming and wishing it could be several more grown children heading over here, too. The memories just picked me up and took me there."

"Been there on several occasions myself. That flood was the worst thing that I've ever seen. I had to make myself find another path and come back to the here-and-now and be thankful for what we still have." He reached down with his hand and pulled Lottie's face upward toward him. She smiled and blinked hard against her tear-filled eyes. "I'm back. The trips probably will never stop, but they get further apart. I guess time does heal…a little anyways. This is the first porch since that time that I enjoy sitting on. Dugan Holler is healing me."

The light from August's and Henry's car lighted up the porch. She and Henry got out. Jake was with them.

"Happy birthday, Momma." August yelled. "Did you remember, Papa? What about you, Norabell?"

"They all remembered," Lottie said.

"I sure am glad it quit raining so hard. I think the stars are trying to shine." August reached inside and pulled out a chair.

"Come on Henry, I have to go to the barn and check on something," Beck said.

August motioned to Jake. "Go on in, and find Norabell."

Beck had been to the sale barn in Lawrenceburg and had come back with a sow and boar hog.

"I wanted you to see what I bought. When we have a litter, I'll give you and August one to fatten up to kill. Ham and hog's jowl will taste mighty good."

Beck took out his knife and made a small notch in his fingernail right at the edge of the skin.

"What are you doing?" Henry asked.

"I put a notch there and, when it grows out to the end of the nail, it will be exactly the time it takes for them to be born. A little over three months. I'll know when it's getting time and put in some hay for her to have them, so it won't be in the dirt or mud."

Two hens and a rooster cackled and ran from the barn.

"More chickens I see." Henry laughed.

"Lottie says she can trade eggs for about anything that a family needs to eat. Also, a man doesn't need a clock when he's got a good crowing rooster." Beck shooed them into the chicken house and closed the door. "Before we're finished, I plan on us being completely able to feed ourselves and take care of our own needs...and our family, or course."

***

Ten minutes after Jake arrived, he and Norabell came out and stood in front of Lottie and August. "We've got some news."

Lottie and August turned toward them.

"Well, do you want to know what it is?"

Lottie nodded. "I figured you'd spit it out when you got up the courage."

"We plan on getting married! Jake asked me the other week, and I said yes."

"It's what I expected." Lottie looked from Norabell to Jake. "Do you know what you're getting yourself into, Son? She's pretty spoiled. The baby girl always is. Not that I did it all by myself. Beck and August have done their part as well as the rest of the family."

"I'll do my best to keep her spoiled just like you give her to me."

They laughed.

"If I can, Momma, I'd like a little wedding." Norabell folded her hands like she was praying.

"I'd love to give you one, but it may not be possible.   Extra money is slim pickings right now. The war is hurting us all." Lottie stood to hug her.

"It don't have to be much...maybe a new dress and some yard flowers. We could have it right here in Dugan Holler.

Hmm...a dress?" Lottie looked at August and waited for her nod.

August swallowed the knot in her throat. "Baby girl, I have my wedding dress. Actually, Momma has it in her chest. I begged her not to give it away or cut if up for other sewing projects. I had hoped you would want to wear it.   We'll get it out next week when I come over.   I was about your size when I married, and it won't need much sewing unless you want to change parts of it." She walked over and stood by Lottie. "Momma made it for me. She let me have a whole week's pay from my work in the mill to buy the material at the store. It may have yellowed a bit though."

Lottie put her hands on her hips and looked Norabell from head to toe. "It'll need a bit of stitching. Norabell's waist seems a little tinier than yours was, but I can fix that in a moment."

"I don't mind the yellow that comes with age. It just makes it more special knowing my sister wore it, too. You have a happy marriage. It will surely bring our lives together, and we'll be happy, too." She put her arm through Jake's and looked up at his smiling face.

Jake rubbed his hand on his pants. "I was a little nervous coming with her. If you all don't mind, don't say anything to Beck yet. I haven't properly asked him for Norabell's hand. She couldn't stand it another minute and had to come to you two first. I think I'll leave you ladies together. Beck and Henry went to the barn." He leaned toward Norabell but jumped back when she put her face up to kiss his red one. Instead, he stuck out his hand for a shake.

The women roared with laughter.

Lottie said, "Go ahead and let her give you a little peck on the cheek. You didn't think we had never imagined you've kissed her before? Just make it quick, and get out to Beck before he comes in. It's our secret that you told us first. You know Beck wouldn't like that at all."

Norabell did a tiny jump and headed to the other side of the porch to watch until Jake faded into the darkness.

Lottie grabbed August's hand and pulled her inside the house.

"Being together with the dress would make a perfect time to do some explaining. It needs to be done."

August pulled her bottom lip between her teeth and chewed on it. "I don't know, Momma. Some things are best left in the dark corners of yesterday. They don't help nothing and can be a tad bit troublesome."

"Trying to talk yourself out of it, are you? Every day you wait is another day she'll hate you for it. She'll find out. It won't remain a secret forever."

"Hate me? Why not hate you? You could have told her this a long time ago."`

"I told you, August, that if there was any talking to be done, you'd do it. And I reminded you that the day would come when you couldn't put it off any longer. That minute is fast approaching. Get your thoughts together, and open your mouth."

"I will. I will. Soon, but not today. She's too happy right now. Let's don't spoil it. "

August glanced out of the corner of her eye and saw Norabell coming toward the door, and quickly changed the subject. "Momma. Wasn't this about the most surprising birthday gift you've ever had? I want to take you to town tomorrow. The dry goods store is having a sale. We'll find you the prettiest dress you ever had. You can save it for the wedding if you want." She looked to Norabell. "Have you set a date?"

Norabell twisted with excitement. "We think next month. A fall wedding would be nice. Especially if we have it out of doors. The leaves will be turning, and that'll add color." She turned to Lottie. "We got into this house just in time to plant flowers. I bet those seeds August gave you to plant for the fall will be in full bloom. Let's have it in front between the porch and the water. We could cut the flowers in the back yard and put them in fruit jars and sit them all around."

Lottie nodded in agreement, then stopped and took a deep breath. "But where are people going to sit? At least in church you'd have pews. I love a church wedding."

"Churches are nice, but I want it here. Dugan Holler is the place where I lived when I fell in love. People don't need to sit. All the weddings that I've been to don't last fifteen minutes. They can stand that long, surely."

August and Lottie laughed.

"She's not too concerned about her guests, is she?" August shook her head at the excitement of youth.

Lottie said, "I'm sure your daddy can hammer a few planks to some sticks of wood to make benches. How many people are we talking about?"

Norabell started to count on her fingers. "All of the family that live here. A few friends from church. PeNellie and her Mamia, if they'll come...."

"Never mind. We'll figure it up later. Good thing Momma and I canned a lot of food this spring from my two gardens. That should take care of the food. We can take planks and put them on saw horses for tables." August turned to Lottie. "I have a few tablecloths, and the ladies at church would probably let us borrow some more."

Lottie raised her hand and waved off August's thoughts. "Don't worry about that. We can use sheets."

Beck, Henry, and Jake walked in the door.

"I have a feeling you've already heard that our baby wants to get married." Beck shook his head at their excited faces as they planned the wedding.

They all laughed.

Norabell ran to Jake and pulled him back on the porch.

August gathered her things and walked to the front door.

"There's no need to run. I'll just find you and say what I have to say anyways."

"I know that's the truth," August snapped. She turned around and whispered. "There are two kinds of secrets. One you want to hide for selfish reason, and the other you don't dare let anyone know because of what it can do to people."

"A person can try to hide their secrets, but time has a way of bringing all things to light. Secrets are a prison to anyone that tries to keep them. They eat away inside while you bite your tongue whenever you accidently blurt something that tells there is something you are hiding. It makes a person lonely and separates them from things that are good. You also have to think about those that you're keeping the secret from. Do they have a right to know? If it concerns them, I think they have every reason to be told."

August pushed her lips tightly together. "Sometimes secrets protect people. Everyone has a right to keep silent on things that are not anyone else's business."

"You think this is not her business?" Lottie laughed but not from humor. "Is it really her that you want to protect? And from what? Or is this about guarding you and your friend? If it's about us, I think we're big enough to shoulder the responsibility of our actions. If things had gone like we first thought about handling the problem, she might already know."

"Or she might NEVER know. Can we stop talking about this? I'm the one that will decide if or when we tell her."

Lottie folded her arms. "So you think you're the only one this affects? This secret has more arms than a hay rake. She could hate us all before this is over and done. Even poor, dead Maggie."

"So, I can't get a clear take on what you are saying. Do you want me to tell her or NOT? Can you straighten that out for me?"

Beck came over where they spoke softly by the door. "It's a good thing Jake is letting Norabell talk a mile a minute. If not, she would hear every word you both have said. Is this how you want her to find out? Go home, August. You two do not need to be together right now. Think about this, and talk later."

August's eyes filled with tears. "I'm sorry, Momma. I just don't know when or how to talk to her."

Lottie placed her hand on August's arm and stayed silent.

***

There was nothing Lottie liked better than her time alone with Beck. Especially if it was a foggy morning, with a light, off-and-on drizzle, and they could sit near the water.

Lottie crossed the foot log and sat down on a stump. She watched Beck stride in long, even steps down to the creek. He was surefooted and smooth in his walk. His face was long and angular with high cheek bones. The only way age had affected him so far was in the silver that replaced most of his dark hair. It still curled around his ears and the nape of his neck. For once, he had left his hat in the house.

He sat down, and Lottie handed him a cup. They sat quietly and drank their coffee, both deep in their thoughts of the past and of the future.

Lottie turned to Beck. "I know there's a lot of things that are a burden in this life. It doesn't matter if you are rich or poor. Trouble is no respect of person, I reckon. I always thought that if I had a house like this, that things would be perfect. I know now that's not true. Nothing is ever completely perfect in this life. It's like the cream on the milk from our jersey cow. When it comes out, it's all muddled in with the milk. Let it sit a bit, and the cream rises to the top. When you think about life in general, the good gets all mixed up with the bad and everything seems bad for a spell. If you sit down and get your mind on it, you realize that the good is right, and it will rise to the top if you choose to look for virtuous things.'

Beck smiled and shook his head. "I never could understand how you think such deep thoughts and then spring them on me at odd times. You're quite the thinker."

"Something about the quietness of the morning does that to me. Things are hardly ever quiet around here, but silence makes us go inside of ourselves and take stock of our life."

Beck took a sip of coffee and swished it around in his mouth. "Yesterday, after I talked to people in town, I thought about how I used to think about people that moved into the mountains. Outsiders. Now, we are those people. We have come into this part of the country and bought land. Cut their trees and planted crops to compete in their market to sell our harvest. There's nothing that will make you more accepting of people than to become that outsider one time in your life. The world is changing faster than I can get a grip on it. The young men are going off to war to foreign lands. They won't come back the same...if they come back at all."

She nodded. "All these boys dying. Our own grandsons might have to go over the seas. Sugar, coffee, and even gas are rationed for the sake of this dear country. But, even in the midst of it all, I'm happy. Everything passes in time. Bad finally goes away for a spell, and good comes in its stead. It's life. But, all in all, life is good if you'll let it be and open your eyes and heart to it."

Beck smiled. "You're in quite a mood today, aren't you? Rain has always done you this way. It carries you inside, and you think about things deep inside."

"There are too many things to do when it's not raining. It don't give you time to do very much thinking. There are things that may get messy with August and Norabell. That makes for more troubles. In my early years, I'd have been beside myself with fear. If there's one thing I've learned, it's that time has a way of making things right. I just hope it's that way with this. All these years, we've been living a lie."

"I don't want you to worry about August and Norabell. The time will come when those two will have to work it out between themselves. They're grown women, but they won't forget that they are family. There may be some harsh words said, but in the end, they won't forget they're kin. If we have taught them anything, I would think it's that family comes first in life. Nobody else will love you like family, and if you need help, you can count on each other."

Lottie sighed and looked around her at the beauty of the woods. "I'm the happiest I've even been. Living in this holler. Who'd have thought we would be able to buy such a good piece of property. Do you remember how rare it was to have good bottom land in the mountains." She laughed. "I thought people must be rich if they owned land like this. If it wasn't for that blue smoke which twists up from the neighbor's fire from their cookstove, I could feel like we're living back in North Carolina. When we lived in the mill towns, I felt like I couldn't breathe. I was never at ease unless I could feel the trees on every side of me. In town, it was like there wasn't enough breath to go around." She leaned over and laid her hand on Beck's arm. "I'm so thankful for a man like you and all your kindness. I'd venture to say that not many people get to build a house in the midst of a war, but you have. For me. We're old, and our time is not much more for this earth. We work hard...after we get our stiff bodies out of bed." She laughed. "But I plan on being happy what time I have left. And make you happy as well, if I can."

"You already have made me the happiest man on earth. Let's finish our coffee and start working so we can finish paying for this dear land and house, my wife. It's something we can leave our children. They worked hard most of their life too. If I can make it easier for them, I will. Every day, I can feel age creeping up on me. I have to work while this body is still able."

Beck reached out his hand and pulled Lottie up from the stump. "I've begun to believe that all those things I learned to do in our hard times are going to work for me and help pay off this place faster than we first agreed. August and the others said they would help me get out the word that I can cut hair. Henry's papa has the tools for a blacksmith shop that he's willing to sell me real cheap. I can turn horseshoes and shoe a few horses on the side. There's not many things that I can't do when it comes to metal work. Even in war times, people have to take care of their livestock, and most want to have a good haircut every so often if they attend church."

Lottie raised her eyebrows. "Why does Henry's papa want to sell the blacksmith shop? I'd think he'd still need it in these hard times."

"I'm sure he could use it, but sometimes there are things more important in a man's mind. Henry's younger brother is in the army. He was wounded in Europe, and they sent him back to the states. His wounds are so bad that they don't plan to make him go back to the front lines. It seems he can't come home for a visit due to the shortage of gasoline. He could have to stay where he is until the end of the war. Henry and his family want to get money to him so he can buy gas rationing stamps on the black market and get someone to bring him home.   It may be the wrong way to get it, but I'm not sure I wouldn't do the same if it was one of our sons."

Lottie threw the last of her coffee in the water and walked across the foot log. Beck gulped his last drink down.

He fell in step with her. "My plans are to encourage Norabell and Jake to live in that older house that we've not rented. I know that our home is big enough for the four of us, but they said they'd planned to live with his parents until they could find a place. I know it's not always good to live near either set of the in-laws, but this would certainly save them from having to live IN the house with his family."

Lottie made a face at him. "Is that why you took me away from my family?"

"It's strange to me how I never think about your first marriage anymore. It's like it was a different lifetime." Beck put his arm on her shoulder. "I took you away because I was afraid you'd die if I left you in that house another day. Your husband would've killed you. It was only for lack of time that he hadn't already. But, then I fell in love with you. The rest of the moves was in order to make a living for our family."

Lottie knew it was true. "My first marriage was a bad mistake. I think Jake is a fine man, but you never can tell. I want Norabell nearby for a time. Later, I'll encourage them to find a house out to themselves...as soon as they can gather enough money."

Chapter 10

Lottie grabbed her purse and handkerchief and left. August told her that she would take her to town to get a new dress. It was a gift for her birthday.

Norabell pulled back the curtain and watched them drive away. When they were out of site, she headed to her Momma's room. The cedar-lined chest sat at the foot of her bed. She knew she should wait until next week when August could show her, but she needed to see the wedding dress now. That chest had been off limits to her since the day she was born, she reckoned. She had always been a 'plunderer' as her Momma had called it. Into everything. Always curious about everything she could see or touch. Today was no different.

She rubbed her hand down the back of the chest until she found the key. Daddy had taken it out of his pocket and hung it there when Henry had carried it in and placed it at the foot of the bed. Norabell had seen him and made note of where it was kept. It hung on a tiny nail on the backside of the chest. Out of sight to prying eyes.

It opened easily. She leaned the top of the chest against the foot of the bed. It smelled of roses. She picked up two handkerchiefs, one from each end of the top shelf, and sniffed. They had been soaked in rose water and kept inside for the aroma.

Norabell took out the long open drawer and laid it to the side. The dress was on top and wrapped in flour sacks. She had worn a dress years ago made out of the same cloth as the sack material that protected it. Stretched out on the bed, the back of the dress was almost as long as the covers. They would need to pull that up at the back and make a poufy thing so it wouldn't drag on the ground, she decided.

Curiosity got the best of her. She got on her knees and looked deeper in the chest.

There were five little baby dresses made of white material. There was another dress that would fit a girl of about twelve. Those had to be from the children that her Momma had lost to death. Tears filled her eyes. She could not imagine having to bury a baby that she and Jake might conceive. It would be more than she could bear. There was no doubt that her Momma was the strongest woman that had ever lived.

After all the dresses were carefully laid back into the chest, she noticed the drawer had two sections. She placed it back where it had been.   It was actually two separate drawers attached to one another. They could slide from back to front and that covered another hidden area. Each was covered with a flowerdy cloth. The material made a hinge for the lids. She slid one drawer toward her and carefully poked through it. There were tiny pearl beads made into a bracelet on a ribbon….tiny, like for a baby. She picked up a necklace that was made from a single strand of pearls, yellowed with age. She carefully put it around her neck.

I'll ask Momma if I can wear this for the wedding. She placed it back. Her finger moved carefully through tiny items; a single band ring made from a piece of polished metal and a hat pin. A brooch lay in the corner.

She opened the top on the second drawer. It was filled with papers of all sorts. On top, there were rationing cards that had just began to be issued...gas, tires, and more.

Below the rationing papers were four post cards from either Lottie's Momma or Papa. The last card came from her Momma's sister, Sugar, saying that their mother had passed. There were tear stains on it.

She picked up the next paper. It was an envelope. It had not been mailed, but probably hand delivered. Across the front was one word. August. *Why would Momma have a letter that belonged to August?*

It had been opened by cutting off the end of the envelope. Norabell blew into the wrapper and, when it opened, she pulled out a single sheet of paper. The writing was very neat and exact. The big letters were perfectly written.

August,

When I met you at the bridge, your news surprised me. I should not have walked away from you without talking to you. I had actually been on my way to find you andMaggie and say that I was leaving to go up north to school. My father has secured me a place in a large college in the northeast.

From the day I was born, my life has been planned. I would be groomed to work in the textile industry like my father. He wanted me to do more than he did, and he knows that education is the key to my future.

Although I was surprised at your news, it does not change my words that day. It would never....

A motor stopped and a truck door slammed. There were voices and laughter.

Norabell's hands shook as she quickly put the letter back into the envelope and made sure the papers from the box were in the correct order. She locked the chest and hung the key back on the nail.

She closed the door and turned just as her Momma opened the front door. Lottie looked at her hand that was still on the door knob.

"Is something wrong?" Lottie looked up into Norabell's eyes.

"Oh no. I thought I heard thunder. I checked to see if your window was open. It wasn't. Are clouds gathering?" Norabell walked to the door and opened it.

"Clear as can be. Not a cloud in the sky."

"Really? Maybe it was when you all turned. Did the truck backfire?"

Lottie bit her lip. "Maybe. I don't remember."

***

Jake and Norabell stepped out of the Lawrenceburg jewelry store at the corner of Locust Street and North Military. Jake had sold his cart, and with the rest of the money his brother had lent him, he was able to buy a ring. Jake would pay him back. It was probably the least expensive ring in the whole store, but it was what Norabell had wanted. At least that's what she'd assured him.

"Jake, while we have Daddy's truck, let's take a ride out west of town. I hear that part of the county is flat land. I've never been out there. You never know, we might buy some land in this direction someday and farm it." Norabell scooted to the middle of the truck and put her hand on his knee.

He put his arm on the back of the seat and turned to look over his shoulder to see if he could turn out onto the road.

A truck loaded with logs passed by slowly. Behind it was another truck where twenty men sat on benches that had been made on the bed of the vehicle. At the back sat a guard with a gun in his hand. Jake's leg trembled under

Norabell's hand. He dropped his arm from the back of the seat and put both hands on the steering wheel.

Jake shook his head. "I don't like coming to town, and I sure don't want to go out west of town. We don't have no business there."

"Why are you shaking? Your leg is jumping." Norabell looked at him with eyes wide. Her forehead wrinkled.

"Did you see that truck go by with that load of men? It had a guard with a gun in this hand."

Norabell turned around and watched it. "I guess it's criminals of some kind. They probably have been working on the road. We used to see that when we lived in the Carolinas."

"No!!!" Jake yelled.

Norabell jumped at the rough sound of his voice. "What's wrong with you? Have you been in trouble with the law? Is that why you're afraid?"

He looked into her dark eyes. "Those are not criminals, Norabell. They're Germans."

"You mean like we're at war with over yonder? Did they bring them over here and put them in prison in Lawrenceburg? I didn't know about this. Do you think Daddy and Momma knows the enemy is this close to us?"

He tried to swallow the knot in his throat. "The story has been in the Democrat Union. If they read the paper, they've heard about it. These men are from over the ocean. Prisoners of war. But my Papa warned me that he'd heard that sometimes they take Germans from here in the states. People just like us. Those that have German blood, and that's their only crime. The prisoners are working in the woods, cutting logs for building things. They're behind bars the rest of the time. All because they're Germans. If they took Germans from here, it wouldn't matter at all that some of them have lived in the United States for years and others were born here, Daddy said."

"I guess I don't know what is so awful about this. Why does it bother you? We can't be too careful when it comes to being safe. Germans here might want to turn on us and kill Americans."

"Listen to what you just said? I'm part German, and the rest is Scot-Irish. My daddy's parents are full-blooded German. They became as much American as you. Why would they want to kill other citizens? It's not right."

"If you say so. I didn't know anything about these war camps. Why are you so mad? They're not going to take you or your family, and certainly not me."

Jake wished he'd never shown her how upset he was. "All my life, my daddy has said to me, 'Boy don't tell nobody you have German blood in you.' When he read the story of the prison camp in the paper, he told me the same thing again, and he added this time, 'or you'll end up in a concentration camp.' We even changed the spelling of our last name. We use Mince now, but it's really Mintz. The spelling would give us away. Daddy's brother changed his spelling to Mints. Grandma spoke German all the time in our house, so Daddy stopped letting her go anywhere. She died last year. But, according to her, she had died a couple of years before when she was no longer allowed to go among people. She could have refused to do what we asked, but my daddy warned her what would happen to all of us if she did."

Norabell turned white as a sheet. "I don't believe they would take your family or people like you and put them in a prison camp. They'd understand that you were born here. You'd never be like the people of Germany and all the bad things that are happening there."

Jake watched her closely. "Not everyone in Germany is mean. I still have family there. I need to tell you something else. We found out something from a letter from our family that still lives in Frankfurt that a cousin was being held in a prison camp in Lawrenceburg, TN by the name of Emil Mintz. He's the cook for them all he said. We can't dare try to see him. I hope you're right about them understanding if we're ever found out as Germans, but I don't want to take the chance. Not with you and any children we might have. You need to know all about me, though. If you don't want to marry me any longer, I'd understand."

Norabell looked at him like he had two heads and scooted nearer the window on the passenger side of the truck. "Why would that change my mind? I love you. We're going to make a life together. I don't care if we have to change our name to Smith. Let them try to figure out where that last name came from. Why they would hate American Germans is something I don't understand though. It is wrong to hate someone for the birthplace of their family. A person should be judged only by who they are."   Jake was nervous as he watched Norabell lean against the truck door. She'd ridden near him when they came to town. Now she seemed so far away. He jumped when she suddenly turned toward him.

"Jake. This is a whole lot like I tried to tell you about my friend Penelope. You don't like her because her family is gypsy."

He raised his eyebrows. 'That's not the reason."

"Really? Because that is exactly what you said. 'She's a gypsy. Don't be hanging around gypsies. They're strange. They tell fortunes and steal babies.' You said that! I want to tell you that I think that's all poppycock. Just like the fact that people believe that all Germans are out to kill us."

Jake tried to hold back his laughter but couldn't.

"Are you laughing at me?" Her face was almost purple with anger.

Jake reached his hand out and took hers. "I'm sorry, and you're right. I shouldn't have judged her. You're very good for me. Do you know that? What I was really laughing at was you saying poppycock. What a highfalutin girl you are. I've heard silly notions called a lot of things but not poppycock."

She began to laugh. "I heard the word one time when I was listening in on a conversation. I worked at a ladies tea in the Carolinas. I was serving tea when a girl protested to her friend that her parents hated the guts of the boy she was in love with. Her mother overheard her say that, and she said 'that's poppycock'. I almost spilled the pot of tea. I've always wanted to use that word ever since."

All the way home, they would quieten down, then one or the other of them would start laughing again. Anything they said, the other replied "that's poppycock."

Chapter 11

Norabell wiped the sweat from her forehead with her apron. It was hotter than Hades today, too warm for late September. Her Momma had told her if she'd pick enough muscadines, or even possum grapes, for both of them, she'd make jelly on the halves. There would be berries for a pie for most of her and Jake's first winter. Sugar was already on the list for rationing, but Lottie had traded eggs all winter for more sugar stamps. Better make the jelly now before the sugar turned lumpy. The jelly would keep for several years once it was canned. If it turns to sugar, you could heat it and pour it back in the jar.

She looked around her real good for snakes and then squatted to pick the lower fruit on the vines.

Not far away, a horse snorted and a man cursed. Norabell stayed crouched down in the fence row near the road and peeked around the bushes. Punch Carver stood in his yard, and Dawson Gray was in the road.

"Stay off this road, Dawson. You have no business around here."

Dawson cursed. "I can travel this &*%*@* road, and do it anytime I choose. It's a public road. It was here before you or me ever come to this part of the country. Just stay in your house and don't watch me go by, if it's a problem to you."

"What's your business in passing this way?" Punch took two steps toward the road.

Dawson's horse jumped sideways and danced around at the yelling. "None of your bees wax, but I'm going into Leoma to mail a package. This is a public road, Punch. I will need to use it to carry crops to market and a dozen other reasons that causes me to travel through here. None of them are any of your business."

Punch pointed at Dawson. "Elizabeth just left in our truck to go into town. Maybe you have it in mind to meet someone. Maybe her.

If I was you, I'd turn around and go back home. Mail your package some other time or at some other place, and stay away from my family."

"I'll mail it where and when I get ready. Stay in your own yard, and leave good law-abiding citizens alone. Nobody made you God. You can't run everybody's life like you do your family. I can go anywhere I choose and talk to anybody I want to. Did you fly off the handle in a jealous rage like this when you killed my friend years ago?"

Punch explained, "I didn't have a choice and you know it. You were there. He pointed a gun at me. He may have been your friend, but he was a good-for-nothing scoundrel that took things that wasn't his. Turn around and go home, Dawson."

Norabell watched Dawson throw back his head and laugh. "He never took a thing from anybody. He was as honest as the day is long. You always were a jealous so and so."

Punch turned and ran toward the house. Dawson made a clicking sound with this jaw, turned his horse, and rode around the curve. He was out of sight by the time Punch returned.

Punch looked in the direction of Norabell. She jerked back and hid. She wasn't sure, but she thought she saw a gun in his hand. There was no way she was going to look again.

*   *   *

It became common practice after church on Sunday that Norabell went to Jake's house. Later they would meet with his friend, Punch's son and his wife. The couples would go to the creek near the Carver house. When it was warm, they would wade in the water. On cooler days, they sat on the rocks and talked about their plans for the future.

Today, they were on their way to meet them when she asked what Jake knew about past problems between Punch and Dawson. "Why do Punch and Dawson hate each other?"

Jake raised his eyebrows. "I'm not sure they actually hate each other. They just don't tolerate each other very well. Why do you ask?"

"They seem to hate the ground the other walks on." she said. "I saw them arguing the other day when I picked muscadines near Punch's house."

"That's a pretty good distance to walk for muscadines." Jake took her hand and held it as they walked.

"When we visited there the last time, I saw how many was growing there near the road. I knew they were larger and easier to get than the ones near our house. Back to Punch and Dawson. That day they fought over the chickens seem like more than problems with dogs and Dominickers. It has to be much more."

"I heard it started from something back in Cocke County, Tennessee. They both lived there before settling here. It may have been the murder of a friend of Dawson's. The men hate each other, and it's still a bone of contention between them. But now, they fight over that dad-blame road more than anything. Punch threatens to string up a fence across the road, and Dawson promises to cut the wire if he does."

There was so much more that she wanted to ask, but they were at Punch's house. It would have to wait.

***

Jake picked up Norabell and sat her on the back of the truck, then climbed up. She scooted to the front part of the bed and leaned her back against the truck behind the cab. Jake sat down beside her.

Beck got in behind the steering wheel. Before she got in, Lottie leaned around the truck and said, "You two can sit up front. It may be a little cool back here."

"No, Momma, we'll keep each other warm."

Jake jerked around and stared at Norabell. He turned deep red.

"I have no doubt," Lottie laughed. "I can tell this is going to be a long day."

They got to the Nubbin Ridge road and waited for a few minutes until they saw cars climbing the hill. They pulled out, and the car with August and Henry and another couple pulled behind them.

They found a place to park just off the town square. The trucks started to roll through at 9:00 a.m. All through the day, men passed as they returned from the Louisiana area where they had been carrying out war games.

"Look at that equipment coming here," Jake pointed to Henry. "I've never seen anything so big. I wonder what it would be like to drive something like that."

Norabel's eyes got big. "I hope you never find out. These men are somebody's son, and maybe even's someone's husband and a father to some children. It's sad that they have to fight."

"Somebody has to fight." Beck put his arm around Norabell. "If nobody fights, then we might lose freedoms that we love so much. For right now, they're only calling unmarried men, although some are volunteering. Next, they say it'll be married men with no children that they make go. It continues until the war is over."

Tears pooled in her eyes when she looked at Jake. If they were going to get married, they had better make it soon. She hugged her arms around her stomach and looked away from the servicemen going by. It made it feel so real.

Several policemen stepped out in the road and instructed the people to move back and make room for the trucks. Lottie leaned forward and could see more policemen at every intersection in sight.

That day, 3,000 troops passed through Lawrenceburg. The next day, there were 1,100 more trucks, and the day after that 1,400 more were routed through.

Norabell and Jake crowded into the car with August and the others to ride back, three people in front, and three in the back. She didn't want to sit with Jake anyway. Worry made her feel sick. She didn't know what she would do if he had to leave.

Chapter 12

The wedding dress lay on a sheet on the front porch in front of the swing where her Momma was carefully taking out stitches.

"Did you really think I could change a dress just from these pictures you brought from some magazine that your friend had? It's not always that easy."

"You can sew better than anybody I know. You can change that dress like I want it. I have faith in you."

Lottie shook her head and continued to take out stitches. "You always did know how to wrap me and Beck around your little finger. Nobody else can do it quite like you do."

Norabell smiled and sat down on the edge of the porch and leaned back on her elbows. The dark horizon lit up with flashes of lightning. A hint of the fresh smell of rain was carried by the breezes of the night air.

"Momma, me and Jake visited Punch Carver and his family yesterday afternoon."

"Mmmhmm." Lottie mumbled.

Beck settled onto the porch swing beside Lottie and pushed the dress to the side.

Norabell watched Lottie close one eye and try to thread a needle. Beck took it from her hands and did it for her.

"Like I was saying, Momma, Punch Carver and Dawson Gray seem to have grudges. I don't know what it's about, but they sure have aught one against the other. A few weeks back when I was picking muscadines, they got into it something awful near where I was picking. They didn't see me, because I hid behind some bushes. Punch told Dawson not to be coming down the road in front of his house. He said that, if he kept passing by, there was going to be a fence across the road soon. How could they hate each other that much?"

Lottie pushed the needle through several stitches but did not pull it through, and laid the dress to her side. "It's gotten too dark for sewing. Baby Girl, there are lots of people in this world that don't need a good reason to be mad. They have lots of hatred and anger all built up inside of them. It's got to come out, so they'll find somebody to take it out on."

"Jake said that if there was a fight that he knew Punch could win."

Lottie laughed. "A wolf can take on a skunk, and probably win the fight, but it might not be worth the stink."

August laughed.

Beck linked his hands and put them behind his head. "We knew both Punch and Dawson, and all their families, from when we lived in Cocke County, Tennessee a bunch of years ago. There was bad blood between them even then."

"Daddy, she don't need to hear all that trash from the past. Some things are better left behind." Lottie elbowed Beck.

Norabell sat up and turned around. She pulled her knees up and smoothed her dress over her legs. "I want to know. There must've been something bad that happened." She kept what Jake had said to herself. She wanted to see if his and her Daddy's story matched.

Beck started to rock the swing back and forth with this heels as he talked. "It happened before we moved to Newport as I remember people saying.   The two families were neighbors.   When we lived there, our house was about three-quarters of a mile down the road from Punch's family.   There had been a murder.   I think it was about three months before we moved in. I never did get the exact story, but one of the two boys...I think it was Punch...killed a man by the name, I think, of Stapleton.   He didn't go to jail because he claimed he only did it because the man threatened him with a gun."

Lottie said, "I thought it was Dawson that shot him."

Beck shook his head.   "Supposedly, Dawson's family were close friends with the man that was killed.   That side said it wasn't so...that the man never even carried a gun. They claimed he only had a rifle for hunting for food for this family, which he kept at home, and he wouldn't hurt a fly, otherwise.   The anger just stuck in Dawson's craw, and he never got over it.   Seems like it's still going on. Punch was put out that people accused him of murder."

"That's enough bad news.   I've had plenty of that for a lifetime.   Let's talk about something good."   Lottie folded the dress up in the sheet, laid it to side, and stood.

Norabell looked at her daddy. "If they hated each other so much, why did they move so close together when they came here?"

Beck laughed. "That's a good question. I think one bought land from a land dealer and the other is renting. Neither thought to ask who their neighbors would be."

Lottie rocked back and forth. "Let's stop talking about this, please."

Beck continued like he did not hear her. "I remember telling Dawson's Momma that she needed to teach her children to forget. They both knew the only way to stop the feud that was festering between them was move away. Get away from the reminders that smothered them every day. It was a cruel stroke of fate that brought them back together."

Lottie walked to the edge of the porch and looked up into the sky. "Ain't them stars something? Just think, all my children back in North Carolina might well be looking up in the sky right now, too. We see the same thing."

"No Momma. I want to hear more. Is there anything else to the story?

Lottie turned her eyes sharply at Beck. He stood up and went into the house.

Norabell put her hands on her hips. "Thank you very much, Momma! All I wanted was to understand why they hated each other so much. Is that wrong?"

Lottie sat down on the porch step beside Norabell, and stayed there quietly for about ten minutes. Neither spoke during that time.

Lottie took a deep breath and finally said, "Norabell. I came to Tennessee because all I've ever known in the Carolinas was revenge, bad blood, and sorrow. You've heard Beck tell about my first marriage and how I was slapped around and kicked all the time. I've also had more babies die than you can shake a stick at. The one thing I wanted when we moved here was to leave it all behind, as best I could, and have a good life in Dugan Holler. I can't bring back my babies as much as I would like to. Talking about it only makes me feel all that pain over and over. Things are often better left in the past where they belong or they hurt you all the time. The only way to do that is not think about it all the time and not study about the matter."

A star shot across the dark sky. "Make a wish Momma. A shooting star is lucky."

"My wish is to be happy...to be free from the sorrow of my first years."

Norablle wrinkled her nose. "I don't think you're supposed to say the yearning out loud."

Lottie smiled. "Lordy, I'm stiff." Lottie had a hard time rising from the steps. In the distance, a panther squalled out.

A chill went over Norabell. "I hate that sound. It sounds like a woman crying."

Lottie reached down and took her hand. "Walk to the barn with me. The cow keeps bellowing, and I want to make sure there's no varmint trying to get inside."

There was no moon, and the darkness, in spite of the spattering of stars, felt thick...blanket-like. In the barn loft, an owl let out a haunting sound. "Hoooooo. Hoo. Hoo." A second one hooted in answer to it.

Lottie cocked her ear to the side. "The hoot of an owl means to be careful. Papa used to say an owl means someone was going to steal from you."

All seemed well in the barn. Halfway back to the porch, Lottie stopped in the darkness and turned to Norabell. "I've told you about my sorrows and pains, but, before I was ever born, my family lived in the midst of hate and meanness. I know you have heard some of this story, but I am going to tell you more. There was a feud between my Papa's family and my Momma's. It probably started years before they were born. Who knows how long it had been going on? Maybe for generations, clear back to Scotland, so they say. They always wanted things to be 'even', to better the offense with their own payback, if you know what I mean. If I killed your cat, then you thought you had to kill my dog. My Momma's family murdered my Papa's Papa and his brothers and another family member. They put the heads on pike poles and stuck them up in their own yards for their families to see. Terrible things. My Papa was sent away to live with family in Tennessee. When he was older, he came back for revenge. It was during that time that he met my mother and fell in love with her. He didn't know she was a Hooper. Me and my brothers and sisters are the result of that union of love."

"You never told me that story before." Norabell leaned her head on her Momma's shoulder. "I like love stories."

"Well, it ain't a love story I'm trying to get over. It's that hate and bitterness only create more hate and bitterness. At some point, somebody has to make an effort to stop the fighting. If they don't, more and more flesh and blood are lost, and it's not worth that little feeling of satisfaction that you got with revenge.

Lottie continued, "I don't know how long this feud between Dawson Gray and Punch

Carver has been going on, but I promise you this, one day it will be so strong in one of their heart, that a killing will take place. That kind of hate is not satisfied until somebody dies."

Norabell shivered. "I hope not. I really like Punch. He makes me laugh. I only met Mr. Gray a few times, but he seems a likeable man."

The thoughts of what hate can do made a chill cover Lottie's arms. She said, "It always amazes me that most people are nice when you talk to them one at a time, but they can turn into a crazy person if something stirs up their hatred. It's almost like a demon takes a hold of them. Their eyes flash with evil and the shape of their very face changes, like something takes over their bodies. You watch it the next time when you're with them. See if I'm not telling the truth."

"Hate is a terrible thing."

Lottie nodded. "It's not hate that's so bad. It is a normal thing for hate to rise in a heart at injustice. It's the person that allows that feeling to take shelter in his heart that gets eaten alive by its poison. It doesn't' even change the person that they dislike."

"Please tell me what you know about these men. I heard Daddy's side. I want to hear yours."

Lottie folded her arms. "This thing between Punch and Dawson is nothing but an old-timey feud, but the fight is never only between two people. It becomes a family thing. Everyone expects you to enter into the promise that you will fight together as one. The plan is to fight until that other family either all die or move far away from you. Every incident is meant to cause the greatest loss upon the other side with little harm to yours. So you ambush so you don't get hurt. The fight belongs to everybody. That was what happened between the Hoopers and Watsons. They wanted revenge at any cost."

"What kind of things did the Hoopers and Watson family do to each other?"

Norabell had been a curious child and probably always would be. This question was just typical of her thirst for knowledge. What and Why? She would demand an answer and pester a person until her nosiness was satisfied.

The two women went back to the porch. Lottie sat back down in the swing. "I remember my Momma told me that some Hooper boys, sons of her great uncle, were buying, trading, and very possibly stealing mules and horses to send up north and get them into Yankee hands. They stored them on her grandmother's place up in the mountains without her knowledge. She said Papa's cousins, the Watsons, found out about it and slipped into the field one night and cut off the tails and ears of every one of those animals, about forty of them. That was the last thing that happened before the Hoopers came into the Watson's house and killed my Papa's papa and his brothers.

"I remember when my Papa told me about when they murdered his family. They brought the bodies back to the house to get ready for the burial, then his Momma took out a handkerchief from her bosom and sopped up the thick, blackened blood until the cloth was soaked in it. After it was over, just before she sent him away, she showed him that handkerchief and suggested that the only honorable thing for him to do was, one day, come back and make them pay. She showed it to the children of my grandpa's brothers. They wouldn't listen to her, and only wanted the feud to die. As mad as they were, they knew that you can't bring back the dead by killing another. In all those murders, not one person was ever convicted of it. Grandma wanted mountain justice fulfilled. That was only possible if she could make it stick in their long memory of what had happened. That blood rag was a good picture left in their mind. She didn't care how long it took. Even if she sent my papa away, she knew he'd come back to do a blood revenge."

Lottie said it all as she looked at the darkness around her. "Hate is a dark, black thing that darkens the mind. It tore our families apart. Papa said they were never a close family after that. They barely talked to one another. It doesn't stop with the kinfolk. Hate is contagious, and it spreads fast. Friends and family by marriage are pulled into the vengeance. To make a long story short, Papa found he didn't want revenge. He wanted a family. The marriage of my momma and papa was a hope, to those that found out their connection, to bring the families back together. It has been years, and it still ain't happened. On my last visit, I heard some stories that makes me know it's so. Men killed as they were fishing on the river. Names like Hooper and Watson makes it seem like it's fitting together, anyways. Sometimes it skips a generation and starts back again. I was glad to move away. Hate feeds on memories kept alive by talking about the injustices. Recounting the problems don't change one thing...just feeds the hate, whether it be families, peoples, or nations. Papa never talked about it to me but that one time, but I heard people talk at school and in town...from both sides of the family.

"I have heard people say that it takes a lot of courage to stay in a place where you are marked for slaughter...to stay there day in and day out, never knowing when you might be walking down the road and someone is hid in the thicket, and they'll jump out and kill you. I don't think it's about courage. I think it is foolishness. It don't have to be a move to another state. It can be only to another mountain, as my papa did. Punch and Dawson...one of them needs to move on. Being neighbors was not a smart thing to let happen."

Norabell was almost sorry she asked. It made her sad. Lottie continued, "I told you about this only because you asked. I really want to teach you to forget wrongs. I want you to know that you only keep the good memories and let the others go. Bad memories cause wars to wage on the inside of a person. It never stays inside. Eventually, something brings it out into the open. War brings out the bad in people. I see it in the newspaper that Henry brings home to August. I hope none of our family has to go to this horrible war.

"There are all kinds of wars. Nation against nation. Neighbor against neighbor. Parents against children. Sister hating their sister. It don't take much for some people. The best we can do is to put ourselves in another's shoes and think about it from both sides. That don't happen much in life, it seems. Most of us are doing the best we know how. The rest of them that don't, we leave in the hands of God." Lottie put her arm around Norabell. "There will come a day in your life that you will have reason to hate a person, if you have a mind to do it, or you can let it go and move on with your life. It will be up to you."

Norabell spent many days thinking about that conversation with her momma.

***

Early Tuesday morning, Dawson Gray and his teen age son left home to go into Leoma and have corn ground at the mill. They had barely gotten started when they came to the edge of Punch's land, and two strands of barb wire were pulled across the road and hooked to a tree.

Dawson got down off the wagon, walked to where the wire was fastened, and reached down.

"You had better turn around, Dawson. Punch has promised if you cross this way and take down the wire, he would kill you." Punch's wife yelled.

"Dad. Look coming here."

Punch came out of the back door of the house with a shotgun in his hand. He cursed, then yelled, "You cannot go this way. Turn your wagon around, and go the other direction. If you come across the line where the fence is, I'll kill you." He stopped near a walnut tree about fifty yards away.

Dawson stared at him for a moment, then removed the wire.

"I'm not turning around. This road has been here for years. It was used by the public before either you or me came to Lawrence County. For certain, it was before either of us moved to these farms. You have no right to put a fence up across the road. If I have to go around, it adds ten miles roundtrip to the mill or town. Only a crazy person would ask another farmer to do that, or a very selfish man."

The barrel of the gun raised slightly, and Punch raked his boot through the gravel. "I have every right to put a fence up. I own on both this side of the road and the other. So, therefore, this road is on my land. As of today, this is not a public road anymore. So you and your son just go back. Cross that line at your own expense. A man is entitled to protect his property."

"I'm not harming your property by passing through here. Do you stop any other person that comes this way, or is it just me that you hate?"

A small dog yelped when the rock hit him. Punch tossed up another rock with his right hand.

Dawson looked down at the new puppy his son had brought home the day before. He scooped him up with one hand and held the dog under his arm with its head cupped in his hand.

"Stay right here son with the wagon and the team. I'm going to take the pup home and put him up in the chicken house. I'll be right back." He added under his breath. "I'm not going into this argument unarmed. Stay put. Get down and stand or squat by the backside of the wagon so you won't be a clear shot. You'll be ok. I won't be long. He's as mean as a bear, but he won't hurt you, I don't think."

Dawson glanced over his shoulder a couple of times as he walked to the house, and the wagon and Punch were where he left them. His son had stooped down by the back wheel of the wagon like he was seeing if it was in working order.

He reached out to the door of the chicken house, placed the dog inside, and locked the door. Dawson put his arm inside the back door of his house and picked up his double-barrel shot gun, fully loaded and ready to protect him and his son. He fully planned on continuing up the road to Leoma. There was too much work to be done on the farm to give in to Punch's stubborn block of the road. It would take an hour longer each way if he went around.

The pounding inside his chest continued all the way back to the wagon. He knew if he backed down today, things would only get worse.

He handed the gun to his son and climbed up, then handed the reins to him. Dawson took the gun and laid it across his lap with the barrel aimed in the direction of Punch. He pulled back both hammers and slightly raised the gun. He pulled it tightly against his side and placed his finger on the trigger.

He clicked. "Giddup." The horses danced a little and started forward.

Punch raised his gun.

Dawson knew it was whoever pulled the trigger first that would walk away from this confrontation alive.

The sound echoed against the hills around them.   One shot, then quickly a second one rang out.

CHAPTER 13

Lottie pulled August's body around to face her. "I'm telling you that you need to tell Norabell who her real mother is. I'm not getting a real good feeling about this. I feel antsy. Something is happening."

"YOU are her real Momma. What happened in Morganton is in the past. There's no need to burden her with it." August pulled her arm away from Lottie.

"You know what I mean. I may have always been her Momma, but I'm not the one that bore her."

August's face grew red. "She is to NEVER know that, do you hear? All the way to her own death, it is to be a secret. What good do you think it would do for her to find out about mine and my best friend Maggie's plan, now at nearly eighteen years old? It would mess her up real good. She'd hate you, me, and Maggie."

"She barely remembers anything about Maggie. There might be the memory of the funeral when Maggie died when she birthed her baby boy, but that would be all. And only that because they laid her out in our house because her parents had moved away. Norabell don't have an ounce of bad will in her body. She might be hurt for a while, but she'd get over it quick. There are some things in this world that a person ought to know about themselves, and one of them is who are your real momma and papa. At least by the time you're grown. I've never asked for you to give her any of this news until now. She's about to walk down the aisle with her man, and she needs to understand where she came from."

August bit her lip. She walked to the window and looked out at the tables Beck built that would, in a few days, be spread with all kinds of food for the wedding dinner. There was no reason that she could think of that would make this a good idea. "You promised me, and you promised Maggie, we'd never tell her. Not ever. In fact, it was your idea that we make that agreement." August turned to face Lottie. "Momma, please not now. Not at her wedding. Can't we at least wait a few months and let her get used to living in her own house and not with you. That would make it easier, I think.   Why would you bring it up at her wedding? How do you think that would be of any use to her right now?"

Lottie bit her lip and stared at August. She sat down in a chair and put her hands in her lap. "I guess you're right, as bad as I hate to admit it. I just remember my own wedding day. My momma was right there beside me all the time, right up until I met my man at the altar. It's what a mother does. This should not be me. It should be her momma that tells her all about her wedding night and what to expect of a man after she marries him. I guess she'll have to do with the next best thing." Lottie smiled, but it never reached her eyes.

August laughed aloud. "Is that what this is about?   I don't remember you telling me anything before me and Henry stood before the preacher?"

Lottie fanned her red face with her apron. "I figured you already knew pretty much anything I could tell you. That was the one thing I didn't like about your working in the textile mills. They all talked about stuff in front of you and Maggie that was not right or proper for women to be hearing. They might have tried, even though not very hard, to be out of earshot from you all. They run their mouth right in front of the young girls that were easily influenced. It made you and your friends grow up too fast and messing around with things that girls your age were not ready for. I have protected Norabell as best I could from such bad talk. I am sorry for you having to work like that, but it was the best we could do at the time."

It was August's turn to blush. "Momma, I was twenty-four when I went to work in the section with the men. I was not a young, helpless girl. According to most everyone, I was already an old maid."

A smell of fresh baked pie drifted from the kitchen. "Even an old maid should not have to endure such rough talk among men. And Maggie was younger than you." Lottie stood up. "We'd better get back to preparing dinner. I won't say anything now, but there has to be a day, and it not too far away, when we both sit down and tell her together."

* * *

Norabell looked at the front door and wrung her hands. She knew snooping was not the way a good and honest person should act, but she couldn't help herself. There were more letters and documents in the chest. She needed to know if they had anything to do with her.

She waited until she heard both doors slam and the motor crank. She ran to the window and watched Lottie and Beck leave. She sat down and gave them the time she thought it would take them to get to Nubbin Ridge Road. She needed to know they were truly gone.

Norabell took the key from the back and knelt by the chest. She ran her hand across the cedar wood. It was the one nice thing that her Momma owned. It had been Norabell's grandmother's hope chest, and she had given it to her daughter as a wedding gift. Beck had told the story about how she had had to leave it behind when they moved away, but that Lottie's mother had it shipped by train to her when they settled in Clifton, South Carolina.

She rocked back and forth as she struggled with her conscience. She put the key in the lock.

A noise in the yard made her jump. Norabell ran to the other room and looked out the window. The wind had blown up the makings of a storm, and the noise was the open door to the barn flapping back and forth.

The dress was gone, as she knew it would be. She and her Momma had been carefully changing some of the dress for her own taste.

She couldn't help herself. She had to read the letter from Thomas Johnston again and finish it.　Finally, she found where she had gotten to the last time she had been able to look in the chest.

> *It would never….work out. I told my family, and they said the situation does not change my need for an education. They don't understand the persistence of you and Maggie. However, I do believe they are right that I could not advance in the industry if I married this young. For me to be a common mill worker would be uncomfortable, as my daddy is already a supervisor. It would be unfair for you to ask that of me.*
>
> *If there is need for money for the plans I suggested, let me know. That's all the help I can offer.*
>
> *Thomas P. Johnston, III*

Norablle folded the letter and put it back in the envelope. *I'd give my last Grafonola needle to know more about the hateful man that wrote this letter,* she whispered.

She pulled more papers out of the tray one by one. She didn't want to miss anything. Momma had moved the rationing papers to a small envelope. Norabell turned it over. She had evidently emptied an envelope of its correspondence from the bank and used it to keep their stamps. The next were letters from Grandma and Grandpa Millsaps. She wanted to read them, but she would save that for another time. There was still another section of the papers she had not looked in.

***

Beck stopped to let the horses get a breather. He looked up and saw a woman turn and walk up the road toward him. Instead of passing him by and going past the holler, she stopped at the wagon. In one of her hands was a piece of paper and in the other was an envelope.

She tiptoed and looked at the wood in the back of the wagon. "I needed to ask you something, Mr. Radford."

"All right." Beck answered.

She waved the letter as she spoke. "'I'm your neighbor at the bottom of the hill. We've never formally met." She waved the paper again, this time toward him like she wanted him to read it. "I wrote and asked my son that's fighting in the war what to do about getting wood for the winter. He thought that if I asked you, you might could help me. I don't like asking people for anything...I ain't no beggar, but I'm at a loss of what to do. Before my son left, he had gotten what he thought was enough wood up for a couple of winters. We were sure the war would not last longer than that. It seems that there's no end in sight."

Beck nodded and waited for her to continue.

"My son said to ask the people that bought the Dugan Holler to get me up some wood and tell them that he has promised to pay them as soon as he gets back from the war. Do you think you could do that?"

Tears had come to her eyes. Beck knew it had been hard for her to ask for help. "I can do that. I've been cutting up the tree tops into fire wood as we cleared our land. There'll be plenty extra to bring you a few ricks. I'll bring a load a week for the next several weeks until we have enough to last the winter. If your son is not home by then, we'll do it again."

By now, the tears had started to run down her face. She swallowed hard so she could speak. "I don't know what I'll do if he gets killed and don't come home, but I'll find a way to pay you. I promise. Our word is good. You'll get your pay."

Beck felt sick. This could have easily been one of his own children back in North Carolina needing help when their husband was off in the war. "Again, don't worry about that. When he comes back, and he will, we'll settle up then. Until that time, if you need anything at all, you let me or my wife know. There's no way a neighbor of mine is going to be in need while their child is fighting a war for us. Promise me you'll come to the house if you need anything."

She nodded her head and smiled. "I thank you from the bottom of my heart. The wood is the only thing I need. I'm glad you and your family moved here."

***

The horses jumped when Dawson shot. They reared up and then took off in a gallop so fast that his son fell backwards.

"Get up here and hold on. I don't know if Punch will try to get a shot in or not. Let's run the wagon across the wire I took down, and then we'll go on down the road."

By the time they crossed Sugar Creek, the horses were breathing hard. Dawson slowed the horses to a walk. He looked at his son. There were tears in the young man's eyes.

"Do you think he's dead?"

Dawson shook his head. "He wasn't when we left. His pipe flew up in the air, and he got up and ran toward the back of the house. We'll just have to wait and see."

"What about his wife?" The boy asked.

"What do you mean?"

"Dad, I saw her fall with the second shot. She grabbed her belly and fell on the ground. Her face was white as a ghost."

Dawson looked at his son's white face. "I don't think I hit her. My gun was aimed at Punch."

"But she was right behind him. Could one of the shots hit her?"

Dawson looked back over this shoulder from where they had come. "I don't think so. Surely not."

They rested the horses a bit and continued up the road. At the top of the hill, he yelled "Haw! Haw!" The horses started to run.

At the road that led to Dugan Holler, Beck and Jake came out of the woods and stopped the truck before it entered Nubbin Ridge Road.

Beck had stopped to let the wagon pass, but Dawson stopped in front of him, got off, and walked to the driver's side.

"What's the matter, Dawson? You seem in a hurry. Are the woods on fire?" Beck laughed.

"I just needed to tell someone that I just shot Punch Carver. He was at his house. He'd put a fence across the road. I took down the wire, and he threatened to kill me. It was me or him. It's a shame, but there was little choice. When I get to Leoma, I'll have them contact the authorities, and I'll turn myself in."

He got back on the wagon.

Jake jumped in the truck, and they turned in the direction of Punch's house.

Chapter 14

Neither Beck nor Jake were ready for what they came upon when they reached Punch Carver's house. His blood-soaked wife stood by the side of the road screaming for help.

"Punch is in the kitchen floor. He's dead. It was Dawson Gray that killed him. I've been gut shot, and there's a shot in my hand and in my arm." She fell onto the ground.

A car and another truck drove up in front of them. They loaded the wife into the back end of the truck and headed to Lawrenceburg.

The car followed them. Beck recognized them as part of the family of Punch's wife.

The men jumped out of the truck and ran to the back of the house. About three feet inside the back door, Punch lay in a pool of blood.

Jake ran outside, and Beck could hear him retching. Beck came outside, and they both followed the trail of blood to where he had been shot. The blast must have hit him in the face. His pipe lay on the ground, badly chipped and the stem was broken off about one inch from the mouthpiece.

Beck looked back at the house. "He must have run into the house. Probably never noticed when he went by his wife and that she had been shot."

A young man of about fourteen walked up. "I found Misses Carver sitting by the road. She said she came to and went to find Punch. He was laying in the kitchen, already dead. That was all she told me before I went to get help from their family. Is he in there?"

Jake put his arm across the boy's body. "Don't go in the house. He's dead alright."

***

Dawson and his son went to the Leoma mill, had their corn ground, and then came back to the wagon.

"Son. I'm going to turn myself in. It was a choice of shooting Punch or getting shot."

His son began to cry.

"I didn't have a choice but to shoot him if I wanted to live through this. It might have made a difference if I had agreed to go around, but, at some point, I had to stand up to him. There's no way I can tell you what will happen. If he dies, they may find me guilty of murder, or they might agree that I had no choice. Either way, I'll probably be in jail for a time. You're too young to have this saddled on you, but I need you to take care of the family. Make sure the crops are planted and harvested. It's the only way Y'all can survive. Don't go to the courthouse if there's a trial unless they make you testify. If they do, tell the truth as best you know it, then leave when you're through. There are always things said that are not true, and I don't want you listening to that. You and I, and maybe Punch and his wife if they survive, will truly know what happened. Just remember all I've told you. You take the team and go home. Take the long way, and don't go back by there. I'll wait here for the sheriff to come and get me. No sense of making them come while I am at home and Momma having to see it all."

His son left, and Dawson wiped tears from his eyes.

***

The word had gotten out, and people were coming by wagon or automobile. Two deputies walked toward them. "Anybody here see anything?"

Beck shook his head.

"It was Dawson Gray." Jake said.

Beck grabbed Jake's arm. "He wasn't here. There's no way he knows what happened."

The deputy pulled Jake to the side. "How do you know who it was?"

Jake pointed to Beck. "I was with Beck. We were coming out on Nubbin Ridge Road from his place. Dawson stopped and told us that he shot Punch."

Beck left and went to sit in the truck.

"Yeah. Thank you, young man. Dawson turned himself in earlier, and said it was a matter of kill or be killed. The best we can tell, the only person to see it was Punch's wife. We'll have to see if she lives and supports his story. They may have to call you as a witness to what was said to you.   Until then, go on home and remember all that Dawson said."

The deputies went into the house.

Jake and Beck left in the truck.

***

Lottie pulled out the black dress she had worn to her Papa's and Momma's funeral. The same dress she had worn to her children's funeral. It was the only times she wore it...the death dress, she had taken to calling it.

"I hope the rest of the two families let this feud die with Punch."

Beck opened the door and let her walk out in front of him. "One can only hope."

"Do you reckon that anything will happen at the funeral?"

"I don't think any of Dawson's family will come. There's nothing to worry about."

The funeral for Punch was a simple graveside service. His wife remained in the hospital, and it was not certain she would live.

Beck brought Norabell home in the truck. Jake left the funeral and went straight to work on his daddy's farm until dark. He promised to come and get her that night. She had used the excuse that August might come over, and she wanted to be with her family...even though she knew that was not the case.

Beck walked to the barn and shut the door before they left, but did not turn the latch. It was Saturday, and he and Lottie were headed into town.

"Don't you want to go with us, baby girl?" Beck asked.

"I think I'll stay here and see if I can go down to the other house and clean out some. We'll be moving in soon. The wedding is just a couple of weeks away."

Lottie walked into the room. "I can stay and help if you need me to."

"You go to town with Daddy. I think it will be fun cleaning up the house that will be your own. I may take a few things that August has given me down to the house. A woman at church gave me an iron skillet. She had extra from when her momma died and they cleared out her house. There are other odds and ends I want to put away."

"This may take us a little longer than some days we go to town. I have to meet a man and talk about building him a well house." Beck opened the door and pointed for Lottie to get to the truck.

Norabell breathed a sigh. "That'll be fine. I am a big girl, Daddy, about to be married and all. You don't have to worry about me."

Beck smiled and left her standing by the door. Norabell waved to them when they left.

She sat down in the floor in front of the chest. She reached around for the key. She put it between her teeth and moved the sewing kit that Lottie had put on the top.

Her lip turned white as she bit it. She felt like a robber. Not that she took anything out and kept it. She was a thief of somebody's private thoughts and possessions...even looking at this felt wrong. She put in the key and stared at it.

It's not really stealing when it's about me. Some of this is mine too. Nobody has a right to keep something about me to themselves." She reasoned away her feeling of shame.

She turned the key and laid aside the stack of papers down to the letter where she had left off the last time.

The paper was yellowed, and there were a few dark brown spots. Some of the letters were smudged like they had been wet.

Dear Momma,

We are well. Hope you and Papa are the same. Maggie and I are helping Florence as best we can with only one of us working. We agreed she should take all the money for our keep, so I can't send any home. I'm sorry.

A woman came to see Maggie and me today. She's a teacher here in Clifton. She came from New York on some kind of government project to teach in mill towns in the Carolinas. She told us privately that she is a member of and an agent for the Children's Aid Society. According to her, the Society has been around for at least seventy-five years, starting in New York City. They used to take boys that were orphaned from about ten to fifteen years of age and put them on a train that they called an Orphan Train and sent them out. They would stop in towns and let people take children to adopt. Now, she says, they take babies sometimes, too. She has offered to get a home for the baby. She would say it was an orphan. They don't normally take children from here, but she would get them to make it possible. She showed us a paper clipping from her hometown in Iowa. This is the clipping.

She told us we could keep it, and we agreed we wanted you to see it.

Norabell reached down, took the clipping in her hand, and read.

Make A Choice of an Orphan

***Twelve Bright Faced Children
Craving a Mother and Father's
Love, to be
Here Friday***

Five hundred circular letters have been sent out during the past few days to citizens of this community announcing that a number of orphans from New York will be at the Congregational church next Friday afternoon, from which place they will be distributed to homes which have made application for a child. Be certain to be present at that time.

A letter from the agent from Des Moines, who will accompany the children states that these children come from the best

*orphanages in and around New
York and have been diligently
trained and selected with care to
fit the new family life into which
they are to enter. If a mistake
has been made in the choice, or
for any reason the child be not
satisfactory, the society bears the
trouble and expense of its return.*

*In all there will be twelve
children ranging in age from ten
months to thirteen years. Their
names are as follows:*

*Violet Little, 8 years; Kate
Barnett, 12 years; Ansel Barnett,
11 years; Thomas Steadman, 2
years; Wilheim Elliot, 8 years;
Joseph Harriell, 4 years; Virgil
Lindsey, 3 years; Elizabeth
Golden, 10 months; Margaret
Golden, 10 years; Anna Marie
Honeycutt, 11 years; Edward
Stroup, 13 years; John David
McMann, 11 years.*

*If you apply for a child you
should be prepared to satisfy the
Society that you will furnish the
comforts of home, that you will
treat the little one as a real*

member of your family by taking the place of father and mother to him as nearly as possible, that you will give him the education and moral training that will fit him to take a respectable self-supporting place in the community.

The local committee appointed some time ago are as follows: C.M. Robins; Dr. D.T. Jamison; Judge T.M. Gallaher; M.A. Marshall; Dr. L.H. Johnston; A.C. McCallister; and T.D. Moore. These gentlemen are requested to be present at this time, and it is necessary to have the committee's endorsement when taking one of these children.

Remember that everybody is welcome to call at the church at the above mentioned time, see the little ones, and if you want to do some real good in the world, make application for one of them.

Norabell dropped the paper clipping on the chest at the sound of voices outside. They were back early, and she hadn't even heard the truck. She quickly folded the letter and put it back inside. With one sweep she shut the top and rushed to sit at the table.

She put her head in her hands as they walked in the door. *Shoot. I forgot to put the key back.* She thought. *And I didn't get to finish that letter!*

Chapter 15

Norablle rubbed her sweaty hands on her old dress she had laid on the bed.

"Momma! Come help me get this dress on. I'm afraid I'll pull out the flowers in my hair. August has them sticking in every direction."

Lottie opened the door and slipped inside. "Hush, just about everyone is here and outside. They can hear you yelling. The kitchen is hot. The food is on the stove staying warm." She reached out and picked up the dress. "Put it over your feet."

Norabell sat down on the bed and stuck out her feet.

"Wait until I get a sheet and throw it on the floor. I don't want this dress all dirty before you walk out the door. Once I get it on you, it'll

be fine. Thank God, it don't drag the floor like
I've seen some a-wearing."

The dress slid over her feet, and she stood
up.

"It will take forever to button it." Norabell
tiptoed and looked in the mirror at her hair.
She poked flowers deeper into the small curls
that August had bobby pinned on top of her
head.

"Forever is a long time, baby girl. I'm not
as nervous as you are. I'll have it fastened up
lickety-split."   She smiled at Norabell. "Don't
you let Jake pull off any buttons tonight when
he takes it off."

Norabell turned bright red. "Momma!"

Lottie laughed.

August slipped inside the door. "What are
you two laughing about?"

Two big eyes turned to Lottie. "Don't TELL
her."

"I was teasing her about Jake taking off the
dress tonight."

"Momma!"   Norabell turned to August.
"Can you take her out of here?   I've never
been so embarrassed in all my life."

"The day ain't done yet." August laughed.

Lottie slipped out and left August putting
more bobby pins in Norabell's hair to hold the
flowers.

August secured the last flower and leaned over Norabell's shoulder. They looked at each other in the mirror. "Do you have any questions you want to ask, Baby Girl?"

She shook her head hard.

"Stop shaking your head. You won't have a flower left."

Norabell looked into the smiling eyes of August. "I don't know enough to ask no questions. It came to me that people have been marrying and giving in marriage for centuries. They eventually figured out anything they needed to know. We can probably do the same."

***

The roaring in Norabell's ears stopped when she stepped out of the house and looked at Jake standing with the preacher. She looked at her feet as she stepped down into the yard. At that moment, a violin started to play a soft, gentle tune.

Her daddy stepped up beside her and offered her his arm. She smiled at him, and he reached down and gave her a kiss on the cheek. He stayed long enough to whisper, "Are you sure he's the one for you? If not, all you have to do is say the word, and we'll turn around and go back in the house. I'll send everyone home and nothing else will be said."

"Oh, Daddy." She pushed her shoulder again his. "He's the only one for me. I love him with all my heart. Just like Momma loves you."

"Ok then. I guess I'll take you to him and give you away." There were tears in Beck's eyes.

"Don't you go and cry on me. It'll make me cry too. Weddings are not for tears. They're for laughter and fun. As for giving me away...You're NOT giving me away. I'll always be your baby girl. If Jake would let me, we'd live right here with you and Momma forever."

They took a few steps toward the people. 'No. It's only right that you make your own home. I'll be happy with you having a family that you can bring over any time, though. This new house in Dugan Holler needs laughter of children." He looked down at Norabell.

She smile at him and nodded.

***

Norabell rolled the barrel with a wooden wheel that Jake had brought with them. She loved the small house where she lived near her Momma and Daddy. The barrel was handy when she wanted to carry something to Momma or bring something home.

"Momma, you said I could borrow the wringer daddy got you. I need it today."

"That's fine. You know today is not my wash day. I'll help you load it."

When Lottie leaned over to place the wringer down, a string fell from her bosom. On the end was a key. Norabell knew it was the key to the chest where she had found the letters. She had held it in her hands. She didn't have a doubt.

Lottie reached up and placed it back down the neck of her dress, and it dropped between her breasts. She never looked up.

Norabell thanked her and rolled the barrel back to her house. She felt sick to her stomach. She would not be able to see if there was anything else there about her.

***

Beck drove into the creek and stopped. The bucket he picked up from the bed of the truck had a bar of Lottie's lye soap and a rag. He scooped up a buck of water and rubbed the rag into the soap bar until the water had a film of suds on the top. He washed the truck, threw out the water. The final step was throwing clean water from the creek onto the truck to rinse it.

The truck crept slowly up the hill and was dry from the heat and air by the time he reached the main road. Light rain had settled the dust but not enough to muddy the ruts.

The Democrat Union, the local paper, had announced that the case where Dawson Gray had killed Punch Carver would be heard today. Lottie had agreed, actually encouraged, for him to go into town and watch the proceedings. Knowing them was only half of their interest. After all, this was close to home for the life of a farmer. Could a person legally block the road and have the courts say it was acceptable. Was it murder or self-defense?

Beck arrived on the lawn of the courthouse to watch the court story unfold. At that time, Chesterfield Canton, lawyer for Dawson, and the district attorney came out and stood among the waiting people.

The district attorney held up a hand. "Quiet, please. We have exhausted our supply of possible jurors and are short five people."

A man from the back said, "I thought there were two hundred called to report. That's what they said yesterday. Do you mean to tell me that you can't find enough men out of that group? "

The loud talk started again, and Lawyer Canton waved both arms for them to hush. "It is a slow and tedious job to weed out people so that this man can get a fair trial. We've been ordered, however, to choose five of you." Hands went up in every direction.

Beck kept his hands under his arm pits and waited. The two lawyers darted in and out of the crowd. One of them grabbed Beck by the arm. "You may go inside. You'll be sitting on the jury for this trial." Four others were chosen and led with him into the courtroom.

The foreman of the jury shook each man's hand and assured them that they could work together to hear the charges against Dawson Gray and to give him a fair and unbiased trial.

***

The next day, Beck was standing in the courthouse when the other people on the jury arrived. He had never watched a man being tried, and he was anxious to see what court was like.

They had been seated less than five minutes when Lawyer Chesterfield Canton came in with Dawson Gray and sat to their right. Behind him was the District Attorney. He sat further away and flipped through papers that lay in front of him.

The judge came into the room and spoke directly to them from his seat. "You are the appointed jury for said Dawson Gray, having been charged with Murder in the First Degree in the death of a Mr. Punch Carver. It appears that an extra venire is needed, and I've ordered that the Jury Box for Lawrence County, Tennessee be brought into this open court. Two-hundred names were drawn by the hand of a boy under the age of ten years. Some of you were chosen from that group. They exhausted that group, and I ordered that five more men be summoned from bystanders to complete the group. That, Gentlemen are the rest of you. You will now be sworn in whereas the State of Tennessee is the Plaintiff and Dawson Gray is the Defendant. You are here to render a true verdict according to law and evidence." At this time, the State stated he was "Ready" as did the defendant's counsel.

The judged stopped and glanced in the direction of the jury. "I can also tell that you, as the jury, will be here for several days. You'll not be able to retire to your homes at the end of the day. Gentlemen, there's a room at the jail with several beds in it for your resting needs. If you think you need a change of clothing, please give a list to this gentleman here beside me, and he'll see that your family is notified. They may bring or send you extra clothes and toiletries."

After a few moments, the Attorney-General (Pro-Tem) read the indictment, and the counsel for the Defendant stated "Not Guilty".

Beck had to say he learned more about words and their meanings today than he did in a lifetime up until this moment.

They handed each man a pencil and paper and asked them put their name on it and any instructions to their families and items needed. They were then passed down to the jury foreman.

Lottie would be so surprised, Beck thought. She thought it would be over in a day. *He killed him. He's dead. How hard will it be to get it done with?* She had said.

Beck knew better. First of all, although he had never mentioned the fact, he realized that it was not as black and white as she wanted it to be. Farmers need to get their crops to town and be back to work as soon as possible. He could understand Dawson Gray's reasoning, even if it was not his own. But he had never been faced with the possibility that someone would prevent him from making a living for this family.

It had been two days of talking. The foreman of the jury stood at the end of the table and said, "Gentlemen, we have to make a decision. This is two days we've been here hashing this out. I, for one, want to get home to my family and my business. Let's take a vote one more time. Let's come to some type of agreement."

One by one, they gave their opinions and stated their judgment. Six had given the verdict of guilty and five for not guilty. What Beck was about to do would not make him on anyone's good side. He spoke slowly. "I don't think he's guilty of anything but trying to take his crops to market. Punch Carver had no right to string up a wire across a public road..."

Another yelled, "And Dawson had no right to shoot him..."

There were shouts from everyone concerning their opinion...all at one time.

The foreman waved his arms. "Stop it. We'll just state that we cannot come to an agreement. Then, we can all go home."

Beck held his head in his hands. "A hung jury. What'll they do now?"

"I guess they'll ask for another trial and get another set of jurors to hear the case again.

There's nothing I'd like more than that to happen. I wash my hands of this. I agree with you, Beck. A public road is a public road. He had a gun before Gray went to get his. The one that would live was simply the one that shot first. There was no way this could have ended peaceable. It's been going on way too long for that. It was not whether it would happen but 'when'."

***

The door hit the wall with a thud when Jake came in. "Norabell! I've got some good news. Where are you?"

Norabell opened the back door and stuck her head through. "Back here on the back porch. Momma lent me her wringer today. Your clothes are hard to wash and get clean. They also hold so much water, they take a long time to dry. This wringer should help. Come out here."

Jake brought a chair from the kitchen and plopped it down near the door.

"What's your good news?"

Jake grinned. "You know how your daddy says we need to get out on our own?"

"We are on our own."

He waved his hands at Norabell. "I mean REALLY out on our own. Away from both families. Well, the people that owned the house where the Carvers lived are going to rent it. I get first chance at it."

"The house where Punch died? Are you crazy?"

"I can't help it that he died there. It's a really good house. There are two bedrooms. Four rooms in all. It's not hard to heat in the winter time, they said. All those trees make it cool in the summer. It's near the creek, and there is a swimming hole there. It will be like living in a mansion."

"It's a house where a man died. What if he's still hanging around there?"

"What? Do you believe in ghosts? He's as dead as anybody can be. I saw him. God rest his soul. He'd be happy that we're living there. He really liked you. He told me so once. Let's just try it. We can always come back if we need to."

Norabell took a deep breath. "Alright. If you want to, we will. I may need to talk to Momma and August about it. They've always had second sight. They'll know if it's a good place to live."

"Second sight? I was worried about Penelope putting all her foolishness on you. I should have worried about your family."

He knew he'd gone too far when she threw his pants back into the water and opened the back door. "You don't talk about my family. They get warnings about things sometimes. They don't get a sense or feeling about everything, but enough that I'm sure of their gift. I've never known them to be wrong. I don't think a spirit can hurt me, but it can sure scare me...at least I don't think it could hurt me. I've never met one. But there's always the possibility of a first time. I hope you're the one that meets the haint. It would serve you right." She threw the pants out the door with the water.

Jake laughed, retrieved his pants, and handed them back to her. Norabell wrinkled her nose at him and put them in the tub.

Chapter 16

Lottie met Beck at the door. "Well?"

"It was a hung jury."

"What does that mean? Does he get off free from killing a man?" Lottie walked back to the kitchen where she was frying chicken. "Did everybody think that he wasn't guilty?"

"Some voted that way, and some did not. That's why it was a hung jury," Beck explained.

"Hmph. What's the matter with people? He killed a man."

Beck tried to explain. "You have no idea what happened. It sounded like to me that he shot in self-defense. They had witnesses that told us many different stories about the two of them."

"Well, it sounded like to me from what you and Jake saw that he shot both barrels. Which one was in self-defense, as you put it? His wife was hit, even if she didn't die." Lottie went back to the chicken she was frying and turned each piece that sizzled in the lard. She put the lid back on the iron skillet.

"From what I can imagine, Punch raised his gun, and Dawson shot while he could. I think when Punch fell, the second shot in the double barrel went off. Because he had fallen, it hit his wife that stood behind him. She was further away from Dawson, and the bullet dropped in height as it went toward her. She got hit in the stomach with either that second shot and scatter shot hit her in the hand and shoulder."

Lottie continued to stir the pots of food on the stove. "It seems like a lot of supposing to me. I just know he killed him."

Beck rubbed his hands through this hair. "Don't you think what you contend that happened is just speculation, too? That is the best any of us could do. The bottom line for me was that you can't put a fence across a public road. It's our living that's threatened. Money is hard to come by at any time, but to make it hard for a man to take his cotton to the gin and his crops to market...or even go to the mill to have his corn ground, that's time we could be working for our families"

Lottie put dishes on the table.   She stopped. "I guess I don't have to ask how you voted."

"I guess not. I voted for the farmer that needs to work for a living."

***

Lottie had packed the last of the bedding into Norabell's lap.   "Don't you worry about moving into the Carver house, baby girl. I'm sorry I never got over there this week to see what I felt. August was sick, and I had to tend to her.   It's a good thing for you to set up housekeeping away from both families."

Beck started the truck and drove her to the new house. He had taken his time packing her belongings in the truck so they wouldn't get broken or dusty from the trip.

Jake was already there. He had ridden his horse and led the cow to the small pasture behind the house.

Her daddy had pulled the truck close to the back door. Norabell climbed out of the truck. She put the dishpan full of plates, cups, and silverware in the crook of her left arm and, with her right hand, tried to shut the door.

Jake reached around her and pushed it closed. He stepped back. It was then she saw it.

There was a blood stain as big as the iron tub that Beck was setting in the back yard. The floor was stained. It was also wet with water. Jake had tried to scrub up the reddish black, almost perfectly round circle.

The look they shared was gloomy. They both knew that every time either of them went in the kitchen it would be there. There was no way to get away from it. Punch was dead. He had died right here in the floor. Bled to death they supposed. Norabell handed Jake the dishpan, and sat down on the floor and stared at the blood stain.

"Hey, Jake, give me a hand bringing in this furniture. The clouds are..." Beck stopped and looked from Norabell to the blood stain. "Are you sure you want to move in here? I can just put back what I have set off the truck, and we'll go back to Dugan Holler."

She took a deep breath. "No. We'll move in. Maybe I can hook a rug and put over it. It's over and done with. I have to find a way to cover it though. I can't be seeing it every day, all day long."

Jake patted her arm. "Let's get it unloaded. I can already smell the rain. We'd better hurry."

***

Jake left to meet Papa in the woods. They would be cutting trees all morning and sawing lumber in the afternoon. A knock came at the front door.

Lottie stood with a basket at her feet, a rifle in her hand, and a wagon and team of horses tied to a tree near the road.

"Momma. I 'm so glad you came. Here, hand me that basket. What's inside?" There were tears in Norablle's eyes.

"I cooked your dinner and supper along with ours this morning? We need to put it in the warmer of the stove." Lottie gave her a hug.

Norabell looked at Lottie for the longest time. She looked at the basket in her hands and then to the kitchen door.

"Let's see it. No use pretending it's not there. Beck told me about it last night."

"What am I going to do? It won't come up. Jake tried before I got here yesterday, and I've scrubbed on it most of the night. I got plum sick at my stomach doing it. All these thoughts kept running through my mind. He died RIGHT THERE. His soul left his body where that blood stain is. What was he thinking when he died?

With all that hate, was he right with God when he passed? Oh my...I'm just sick."

Lottie pulled her back into her arms. "You can come back to Dugan Holler. The house is waiting for you. I told Beck you shouldn't be coming to this house, but he would not listen to me. If I had only come over earlier and took a look around, I would have known."

Norabell's eyes got as round as saucers. "Do you think his spirit is still here? Do you feel anything?"

"I don't feel a thing but pity for you having to live here. If I'd only known that he had died in the house. If there hadn't been a blood stain or if we hadn't been acquainted with them, it would've been different. Everybody has to die at some time and at some place.   An awful death like this seems a little different to me. I've been in houses where people had died, and the family had no problem continuing to live where their loved ones took their last breath. But Punch's wife couldn't do it, and I don't know that you should try."

"Jake had to leave with no breakfast. The fire would have had to be started, but I couldn't bear coming to the kitchen this morning. Jake took a couple of day old biscuits and a few cuttings of fat back between them for breakfast. I knew I was an awful wife to send him off to work like that. I know I'll have to do better tomorrow."

Norabell took a deep breath and said, "I'll build a little fire to keep the food warm. Punch's family promised me they'd have electricity put in as soon as it comes to this part of the county, then they'd put water in the house. I don't have the heart to tell them I'm not sure I can last that long." She turned to Lottie with tears running down her face. "What am I going to do?"

"Well...for the time being, you're going to live one day at a time. There's nothing that can hurt you here. Dawson Gray is in jail. He wouldn't hurt you anyway. Punch is as dead as he'll ever be. If his spirit, or something that is familiar with him, comes around, then you just stand up to it. You're stronger than you think. You are alive. You are strong. There is nothing that you can't do if you set your mind to it. I raised you like that. There's no reason for me to think you'll go against your raising. Besides, you'll be busy as a beaver. It will keep your mind off of it. Most every married woman I know is too busy doing housework to do much fretting. As for now, I'm going home and start to hook a rug. Daddy said you thought you needed one. I agree." Lottie stepped across the stain. "Two steps wide, and four steps long. I'll bring the rug as soon as it is finished."

Norabell stared at the gun.

Lottie noticed it and said, "Your Daddy sent this. He wanted you to have a way to protect yourself if you need to." She handed her the gun and a box of shells.

She raised her scared eyes to her Momma's. "Do you think I'll have a reason to use that?"

"I wouldn't think so. A gun does no good in a haunted house, or any kind of spirit, I don't reckon. But it might scare anyone that came snooping around."

Lottie hugged her again and was gone. Norabell stared at the stain for a bit then looked around. "Punch Carver, if you're around here, mind your own business and I'll mind mine."

Chapter 17

"Momma, I brought August's dress back for you to keep it. I have it ready to store back in the chest."

Lottie didn't say anything, so Norabell went into the bedroom.

"The key is in the chest. " Lottie yelled.

Norabell heard an automobile door slam and the front door open. She laid the dress on the bed.

August came into the bedroom where Norabell was folding away the wedding dress and wrapping it in a sheet, ready to put it away.

"I hope my daughter will wear this dress someday." Norabell said.

August laughed. "She'll want to change it some way, just like you did

"I hope you're not upset about that. Momma said it would be fine. We cut it, so I can't fix it back.

August waved her hand. "I don't mind." She turned and slammed the door. "Norabell! I need to talk to you. In fact, Momma says I need to talk to you." August reached over and straightened the tail of the dress. "I remember the day you were born. You was red faced and screamed like the dickens."

August stood up and raised the lid on the chest. "Ain't most babies red and screaming when they come out?"

"I suppose so, but you was different." She pulled Norabell away from her business and motioned for her to sit on the bed. "I'm going to tell you a story about your birth. But to do it, I need you to promise me that you'll not interrupt me. No matter how long it takes. This may even be something that will take days and not hours to explain. Promise? If we stop today, just be patient. I'll tell you everything. This will be hard on me."

"You know how difficult not talking or asking question will be for me. Daddy said my tongue is tied in the middle and loose on both ends."

August laughed. "You get that honest in this family. He once said I was vaccinated with a Grafonola needle."

"Where do I begin? Love is a strange thing. It makes a woman do things against her better judgment and against all things she believe in." She thought for a minute. "I'd like to think it was for love, but in this case, it wasn't love that did it. It was worry. Worry that a person might never be loved by anyone, especially the love of a man. Afraid she'd never have a family of her own. Scared that she'd only have one chance at finding a man and having a home of her own."

August looked at Norabell. "As I said, this may take quite a bit of time…"

"Oh August, do you have to so far back. Just tell me how happy you were to have a little sister. Or are you hiding something in this little story? Why do I feel this is going to change my life? I KNOW you and Momma would never hide anything from me." She smiled.

"What makes you think that we're hiding something?" August's raised up on her tiptoes and back down in a nervous rhythm. She turned around when she heard a noise behind her.

Lottie stood in the doorway. "It's time. No more putting it off. No matter how much we hate to do this."

August groaned. "I guess it is. At the end of a person's life, there are lots of things they wish they'd done different if they could get the chance. Of course, it's not possible. So you just drag your toe in the dirt and make a line. You plan to do things different from then on. Memory is a strange but blessed thing. It's a gift, if it helps make you a better person.

"I think I know what you're wanting to talk about."

August looked skeptical. "You think so?

"I've been going through Momma's chest. Every time she went somewhere and left me here, I went through it. There are some things in there that have made me think they're about me, but I need you to tell me   "

Lottie looked down at the chest. "She always was a child that loved to plunder, August. She got into trouble for that more than anything she ever did wrong."

Norabell smiled. "I never could understand why you would have anything that I could not look at or touch. I wanted to know about everything around me.'

August put her fist over her lips. "You may have gone too far this time. That chest was forbidden to me and every child that Momma ever had. It was the one place that was hers alone. I did not know how that felt until I was grown. There are some things that are none of your business." August shrugged her shoulders, and asked, "What has that got to do with me or my story?"

Norabell's voice squeaked. "There are letters and papers there that tell me something ain't like I thought it always was. But I want to hear it from you and Momma."

"What exactly do you know?"

"I think that I'm not Momma's baby, or I wasn't from the first. I've always wondered about her being so old when she had me. All my brothers and sisters, all years and years older than me. I've heard words about 'change of life baby' from Momma and other people. It wasn't until Jake and I started talking about having a family that I figured up exactly how old Momma would have been when she had me that I started snooping. The wedding dress was in the chest. When I looked inside to get a peek, I saw letters and papers that I read. I waited until I felt you all would not be mad at me for prowling, or for one of you to open it while I was present. I wondered if you would ever tell me if I didn't ask. And, oh, who is Maggie? I think I need to know more about her. Am I right?"

"Well, I see you know some of the story. You're not Momma's birth baby.   The beginning of it all, I'll tell you today. I'm not answering any questions until after the whole story.   I hope in the end you'll forgive me, Maggie, and Momma."

August folded her arms.

"It would be easy to judge a person that gave up a child.   You could think they were trying to protect themselves.   Some would think that it was about not being saddled with a child.   From my experience, it was for the sake of the baby more than the Momma. Children born out of marriage are looked down on. It makes their life hard. Secrets are made and people make promises to never repeat the truth.   A woman goes on about life like she never had a baby, but they never forget. Not ever."

Lottie sat in the rocking chair by the window.   August sat down on the bed where Norabell now lay with her arms under her head looking at them with big round, tear-filled eyes.

"I can help you with this now that you're telling her." Lottie leaned forward.

"No. This is my story, and I'll tell it like I please...not leaving out any details."   August turned to Norabell.   "It's quite lengthy. I'm sure I won't be able to finish tonight."

There was complete silence until August began to talk. "It was 1923 and Maggie, Tom, and me worked at one textile mill in Morganton, North Carolina and Papa and the rest of the family at another one nearby...

"Who's Tom? I read his letter that he wrote to you."

August turned toward Lottie with a red face. "You KEPT that? Why?"

"Because, I knew someday Norabell would ask questions. Just like she is now. I'm not sorry I did it." Lottie returned August's stare.

"WHO IS TOM?" Norabell yelled.

The two other women looked at her.

"Does one of them have red hair?" She asked.

August put her finger to her lips. "Shhh. I'll tell what I can. Don't complain when I do this in pieces. I can't do it all in one sitting. It would be more than I can bear. Let's do it on the next few Saturday mornings until it's over."

There was a light knock at the door. "Are you ladies through putting that dress away? I sure would like to get some rest before having to start at the saw mill in the morning."

August patted her foot. "I know you want to hear the rest of this, but Papa needs his rest. He wouldn't get a wink if we talk in the other room. I suggest we finish this tomorrow after he goes to work. I need to get home to Henry, too.   He's probably wondering if the car was acting up again. I'm surprised he hasn't come looking for me."   She placed her head near Norabell's ear. "I know you don't want to wait, but let's think about somebody beside yourself right now. Let's let Papa sleep."

Norabell rolled away from August and left.

"The bed's all yours, Papa." August said.

Beck frowned and looked at Lottie. "Did you tell her?"

"We started. Got a ways to go finishing it all. I'm still not sure what the outcome will be. She may hate us all."

***

The second trial was much like the first one.   Beck was there on the day the verdict was read.

"Again, we cannot agree." The foreman of the jury read.

Beck didn't realize he had been holding his breath until the air rushed out. It made him feel better, even though he felt, at the time, he had done the right thing. Lottie had tried to convince him otherwise, but she had not heard all the testimony.

A man at his side said, 'They have come in here four times now and said the same thing."

"Well, why don't they call it a hung jury like they did before?"

He shrugged his shoulders. They watched the Attorney General stand up and speak.

"Gentlemen, it is unfair to the defendant to keep bringing him here for trial as it is an expense to him and is a great worry and inconvenience. You ought to decide this case one way or the other, if you possibly can. Please do not keep this case hanging over his head."

The judge nodded. "You're right. It is not fair to be coming back to court after court. It is quite a worry and inconvenience. It is very important that you decide."

After several minutes of silence, the jury filed out again to deliberate.

Beck figured he might as well leave as this could take another day. When he leaned forward to rise, the jury came filing back in.

"Have you reached a verdict?"

"We have, your honor. We find him guilty of involuntary manslaughter and sentence him to 11 months and 29 days in the county workhouse."

Beck turned to the man at his side. "Can they really make them decide? Can't it be a hung jury like before?"

The man opened his eyes wide. "I think they made them give a verdict. They didn't seem to have a choice."

"So what made some of them vote a different way no matter what they believed to be right?"

Beck scratched his head.

***

Norabell and Jake had been living in the Carver house for three weeks when it first happened. Jake set the clock for 3:45 in the morning so he would be up and ready to go when Beck picked him up for work.

The night before, Norabell had cut a few strips of hog's jowl for the morning breakfast. August had given her a ham and a hog's jowl for her wedding.

She watched as Jake left with her Papa and laid back down for a few minutes before starting the day. It was wash day. She really wished she had a ringer washer like her Momma.

She laid there until she felt a lazy streak coming on, then threw back the covers. She put her feet to the floor and reached for her housecoat.

The noise was so loud as to wake the dead. It shook the whole house. Norabell ran to the front room. The back door stood wide open. She would have blamed Jake had she not seen him get in the truck with her Papa. She stuck her head outside. There was no wind at all, so that was not the reason. The sun had lightened the sky until she could see all the back yard, and there was no one in sight.

Norabell stepped back inside. Her foot landed on a piece of wood in the floor. Her hands shook as she picked it up. It was the latch. She was sure that she had turned it to lock the door right before she headed to bed last night. Chill bumps ran up her arms. With one swift push, the door slammed shut. She grabbed a hammer and nailed the latch back on and locked the door.

Back in the bed, she covered her head with the quilt. The house was quiet for ten minutes before she got up the nerve to start her day.

A pile of Jake's work clothes lay inside the bedroom door. Norabell picked them up and put them in a bushel basket. The back door was still shut and locked. She went to the front door, unlocked it and went outside. It would have been easier to go in and out the back door, but she couldn't bring herself to open the door. She walked to the back yard.

The ground was muddy outside the back stoop because it had rained the night before. There were no footprints. With a deep breath, she ran around the house and through the kitchen to the back door. She swiftly twisted the wooden latch and looked out. Whatever had pushed that door so hard, it had thrown the latch across the room. It was surely not human. There would have had to have been footprints.

The words from PeNellie's Mamia echoed in her ears…"Be careful the place you choose to live….For where the bird doth fly, the man will die, in anger he hath left in gall, there his spirit again may call."

Norabell jumped when August spoke. "I brought you a pumpkin and some sweet potatoes."

"You scared me to death." Norabell sat down on the flour barrel. "Don't ever do that again."

"What's wrong? You're as pale as a ghost."

Norabell looked up in fright. "Don't use that word. I have a haint."

August shut the front door and laughed.

"It's not funny. He knocked my door so hard it threw the wooden button latch clear across the room.

August shook her head. "Wind."

"Wind? Did you see a cloud in the sky on your way over here? It stormed last night and this just now happened. It's a clear morning now. It's a haint, I tell you." Norabell took the pumpkin and put it on the table. "And, there ain't no footprints in the mud."

August looked at the back door. "He came in there?" She looked down at the blood stain in the floor, then back at Norabell.

"That's what I'm thinking. It's right where he died."

"Why would he open the door? Couldn't he just walk through."

Norabell glared at August. "I'll ask him next time."

"If it's a real haint, Momma says if you say the Lord's name and ask it what it wants, and it has to tell you."

"I don't care what he wants. He just needs to go on to his eternal destination." Norabell shuttered. "I don't want to think about where that might be."

"But if'n he's back for some reason, maybe you can help him get that done."

"He should have done whatever he needed to do while he was still alive. I want to make him know he is no longer welcome here. He has to GO."

***

Jake found all she had to say hard to believe, but he knew she didn't break off the latch herself. This had happened six different times over the past month. Finally, Norabell came up with an idea to put ten-penny nails in the door...eight nails cross the top and fifteen on the side. The night before, the lock had broken down the middle. It was of no use to keep locking the door with a piece of wood.

"Let's not use the back door anymore. If we have to, we'll board it up from the outside AND nail it shut."

They nailed it shut, and nothing happened for the next three days. It was unhandy to carry things round the house if they needed to go out back, but it was the price she was willing to pay for some peace in their house.

Thursday morning at 4:00 a.m., Jake left for work. Norabell laid back across the bed like she had every day that week. She'd lay there until daylight. There had been no other sound before crashing wood flew across the kitchen. She picked up the rifle her papa had lent her. She ran to the kitchen. She aimed the gun toward the back door but dropped the barrel.

Half of the plank door that held the fifteen nails was still attached to the door frame. All the other boards, including those with the hinges, lay all the way across the room. The nails that held the door at the top lay in the floor, still attached to the broken boards and sticking up through splinters of wood.

Norabell looked through the hole in the wall where the door had been. The trees were black outlines against the early signs of morning sky. Not a leaf was stirring. The curtains at the kitchen window moved as from a light wind.

A large splinter of wood fell from the upper part of the door frame.

She remembered August's suggestion. "In the Lord's name, what do you want?"

"Norabell, don't be afraid. It's me, Punch."

Norabell screamed and ran to the door of the bedroom. She turned around.

"Punch Carver, if this is you, stop it right now. You're already dead. Let the living alone. Me and Jake haven't done a thing to you, and I don't deserve the fear you have put into me. Jake will fix this door one more time, and I think it would be wise of you, for the sake of your injured wife and the rest of the family, that you go on your way to your eternal home." *Wherever that be!* She whispered under her breath. "It's time to let all this trouble die with you and give your family the peace they deserve. I just found out I'm in the family way. It would be a crying shame for me to have this baby in this house with you acting any such way. Stop it. Do you hear me? Stop it!"

The curtains stopped blowing and a peace settled over the house. Norabell grabbed a chair and sat down. She carefully laid the gun in the floor at her side. Her hands shook. Her legs jumped like she was shaking a baby on her knees.

Well, nothing to do but wait and see.

Chapter 18

Beck, Henry, and Jake had left on a coon hunt. Lottie had encouraged them to go. She had whispered to August and Norabell to meet at her house. The three women sat down in the front room of the house in Dugan Holler.

Norabell waited until they were comfortable. "Well…are you going to start or not?"

August leaned forward in her chair and placed her elbows on her knees. "I've gone over it all week. It's as clear as though it was yesterday…."

Morganton, NC
1924

It had rained during the afternoon, and there was mud everywhere. Maggie and August took the long way to August's house...down by the creek and over the upper bridge and back down the other side.

"Well, do you have a plan?" Maggie asked as they came to the bridge.

"For the life of me, I cannot think of one. What about you?"

"I think we need to talk to Tom before we do anything else."

August yelled at her. "I told you I can tell he's not going to do what is right about this. I can tell."

People walking by glanced at the two young women.

Maggie rolled her eyes. "I don't think they overheard anything. Back to Tom. He may not, but we have to give him the chance. We might be surprised."

August looked skeptical but nodded her head. "Very well. We'll wait a day on the family. I'll send him a note to meet us here before it gets dark."

"We'll talk again Sunday before service. Let's try to think of another plan in case he does not..."

Maggie grabbed her hand. "I know."

The short break for dinner was the only time they would have to talk before the day was over. When they got off work, she needed to go home and help with the chores. This was not going to make the others happy. Shoot...she wasn't happy either.

"Let's go down by the water, Maggie." August folded the napkin and laid it back in her bucket.

Maggie followed her down the path to the river. She yelled, "Hold up. You are going too fast. These rocks are slick, and we're going to fall."

August was already down and sitting on a rock by the time Maggie got down the slippery slope.

"I don't have time to waste. We need to talk about this. Today."

Maggie wrinkled her forehead. "We've been too close for either of us to keep secrets from the other. I see your pale face and realize this has to be dealt with."

"I work in the cloth room, and you work in spinning. We're not together in the early morning except on our way to work. There are things that you can't keep from anyone after a time."

Maggie raised her eyebrows. "This morning sickness can't be explained away as a stomach problem each day for a month. Nor can clothes that are tight across the bosom. So far no body has asked about being in a family way. If they had, I would have turned redder than a rose. Maybe even slap their jaws. But when it's known that the monthly visitor has not been around for over three months…that should be the first thought for a person."

August put her arm around her friend. "Well…what do you think?"

Maggie looked worried. "What are we going to do?"

"We need a plan. The family is going to be so disappointed."

Maggie raised her hand. "I have another question. Do we want to tell who the daddy of this baby is? I think people should know. The girl is not the only one that has a baby."

August shook her head. "No, not yet. People never blame the man, but he needs the chance to make it right. A good man will do the right thing. And if he don't want nothing to do with us, I just as soon nobody knows at all."

"You're older and wiser than I am. But do you think he'll be that upstanding man? I'll have to take your word that he has to be told.

Remember when Tom told us how the owner of the mill promised his Papa that he would help send him to school if he comes back and works as hard as his Papa does. But, no, he has even greater ambitions than that. He wants someday to own a mill. Suddenly, there are no longer walks by the creek on Sunday. He doesn't bring a certain girl to the mill and show her all the empty rooms anymore!"

August's eyes widened, and she put her lips tightly together.

"Yes...we both know where it happened." Tears filled August's eyes, and she wiped them off with the back of her hand as soon as they fell onto her cheeks.

August heard the whistle blow. "Run. We can't be late getting back to work. Stay and walk with me home today. We need to make a plan."

***

The girl had on a dark dress. She crossed her arms tight across her breasts and walked onto the bridge, stopped and looked over the side. When she looked up, Tom was walking toward her. He was dressed in a new suit. He had never worn a hat, but today there was one on his head, cocked to one side. He smiled as he came nearer.

"Nice suit." She nodded.

"Papa got it for me. I am…."

She interrupted him. "I'm in the family way, Tom. What are we going to do about it?"

He opened his mouth, but nothing came out. He swallowed hard as though he was choking. His faced turned red. Without a word, he turned and walked away.

***

It was Sunday. The crowd was large for the normal Sabbath meeting, and Maggie and August walked to a tree away from those going into the house of God.

"Well?" Maggie questioned.

"Just exactly like I thought. He didn't say a word…just turned and left me standing there. There was never a doubt in my mind but that he would not do right by me."

"He's a sorry excuse for a man." At the worried look on August's face, she continued.

"Do you remember my aunt and uncle down in Clifton?"

"Of course I remember. She was Momma's best friend. Florence lived next door to us. She and Momma still write to one another." August leaned against the tree and put her hand on her stomach

Maggie continued. "I think we could go and stay with her until the baby is born. Nobody would question you going back to a place you once lived. Have the baby there. You know she'd take us. She can tell everyone that the husband died, and we came there to get away from the place with all the memories. We can let someone adopt the baby."

"You keep saying 'we'. You think we should both go?"

Maggie reached and took August's hands in her own. "We will go together. We are best friends and one of us is always there for the other. Is that not right?"

August raised tear-filled eyes to her friend. "But let someone else raise the baby? How do you let someone just disappear from your life when you've been with them for nine months? I don't know."

"The only other thing that we can do is to the let the people talk all they want. Have the baby and keep it. Eventually somebody else will be the one they're talking about, and they'll forget."

August shook her head. "Maybe they'll quit talking, but they won't forget. It's not just the Momma they'll talk about. It's the whole family. We have to think of something else. Maybe we should go to Clifton."

"It's the only other thing I could think of. When are we talking to our families?"

August grabbed Maggie's hand. "Only a true friend would have said that. It is sad that a person can go a lifetime and never have a true friend like you. Not even one. I feel sorry for them."

They walked back into the church and sat with Beck and Lottie during the preaching.

Afterwards, Lottie was the one to ask Maggie to come home with them for dinner. "I have a ham ready and waiting. I only have to fix the trimmings. We can eat in about an hour."

"I would love to come, Miss Lottie." Maggie squeezed August's hand. "I'll go and let my Momma know where I'll be." She leaned in and whispered, "We'll tell my family after yours."

***

After dinner, Beck left to check on a sick friend. The two of them waited until Lottie was in her chair by the window.

"Momma, would you like to sit on the porch? We can talk."

"Child...you know I don't sit on the porch anymore. I saw too many things from a porch down in Clifton. That is why my chair is now always by the window. It narrows my view. I can choose to pay attention to one thing at a time. I have too many bad memories from a mill-house porch."

"Well we hate to mess up this place too, Miss Lottie."

August frowned at her.

"Am I going to get bad news?" She looked from one to the other of the women. "I think I know what you're going to say. I have noticed you are not eating, August. Every morning you look a little green around the gills. I was hoping I was wrong. You'd think that with all the good Lord shows me, He would have let me see this one coming. But He waited until you told me, I reckon. I guess I don't have to ask who the father is." Tears were in her eyes.

August broke into tears. "I'm sorry, Momma. I can't face Papa." She knelt and placed her head in her Momma's lap.

"I'll tell him." She smoothed August's hair. "Am I wrong in thinking that Tom is not going to be a help through this? No wedding, I suppose?"

August shook her head.

"I'm not good at judging a person either, it seems. But you might be better off that he chose this way. It will be hard, that's for sure. But there are things harder than raising a baby alone.   I lived in that harder way when I married Owen Thompson.   I'm sure you remember at least a little bit of living with your real papa."   Lottie put her arms around the crying August.

"I'm going to give it up. There are lots of people that want babies that cannot have them. I want it to have a good home.   A Momma AND a Papa. Someone to love it."

"I see you've been thinking about this already."

Maggie squatted at Lottie's feet beside August. "My aunt in Clifton will let her come there until it is born. August can come back here after it's all over."

Lottie shook her head. "Yes, she's a good woman. Florence and I write but I've not seen a letter in almost six months. She is just as busy, I am sure."

"Aunt Florence might be able to help find a family for the baby and then August can come back home."

Lottie's face crumpled. "I guess that is a thought." She looked at August. "Do you know how far along you are?"

"Best I can tell, and by all indications, I'm approaching four months. Today was the first day that I was not sick at all. My clothes are a little snug but not tight."

Lottie squeezed her eyes shut, and tears pooled on her eyelashes. "You might be able to stay here a couple more months without anyone suspecting. We can get a train ticket for you to Spartanburg. You could be home in a little over three months. You'll look peaked, so I can say you came home because you were a little sickly. Won't be much of a stretch of the truth after birthing a baby." She pulled the wedding ring from her left hand. "Take this, and wear it. It'll make life easier while you're there."

They were sitting like that when Beck came back a little later, crying and talking. August and Maggie went to take a walk and left her Momma and daddy alone.

When August returned alone, Beck never said a word. He reached out and put his arms around her shoulders. She looked up and saw tears in his eyes. He went to the porch without saying a word.

Chapter 19
DUGAN HOLLER

August rose up and stared at Lottie and Norabell. She quietly went out and left in her car. Lottie watched Norabell. In a short time, she went to the bed and laid down. She had promised Jake she would not stay at home alone.

Inside, Lottie felt like she was standing with her head on a chopblock and the axe would fall at any time. There was nothing to do but go to bed.

***

A few weeks later on a Friday night, the families had gathered at Dugan Holler for their regular family get together.   Everyone had eaten and the men had gone to the barn to look at Beck's new coon dog.

Norabell dabbed at the tears running down her cheeks as she washed dishes. She was the first to speak. "I always felt like there was a part of me that I didn't know. Like something was missing.   Inside, I felt different. It wasn't even entirely about the red hair." She blew her nose.   "Secrets are wrong.   Nothing good comes from keeping secrets. I can't believe that one time I said that I loved secrets! But when it's meant to be kept from you, it's not fun at all."

August dried her hands on the dish towel and pulled Norabell to the table and had her sit down. "In some ways you're right. But as for you, it made your life better. You may not think growing up as a child of an unmarried mother would change things, but you're wrong. It still does and, as far as I can see, it always will. You're not the only child this has happened to. There are probably many people that you know that are adopted and do not know it. Some will die without ever knowing. I have to admit, this was what we planned for you...me, Momma, and Maggie."

August sat down across from Norabell and continued to talk. "The rest of the story is yours alone. I played very little in that part of your life. Except as a sister. By all but one means, you are our Momma's child. She loved you with all her heart. It was because of her that you were not given to another person, someone that we didn't know, to be raised. I think about it often and know that our lives would be so different today without you. Hollow lives, without the spunk and happy laughs that you've brought."

"I lived a lie for years," August continued, "Our family and Henry are the only ones that knew. And Maggie and her aunt. I had to tell Henry. I prayed every day for forgiveness about my lies. Momma and Maggie told me it was for my own good and for yours. There was some comfort with that, but I still felt guilty."

Norabell put her elbows on the table and put her hands up to each side of her head. "If you married, why didn't you and Henry raise me?" Didn't he want me either?"

"I wanted you! But, by then, Momma had already claimed you as her own. It would've been difficult to change anything. When we left to come to Tennessee, Henry wanted you to come, too. He's a kind man. He loved me in spite of my past wayward ways. Most men would not have been so fine. Don't you look down on him. He had nothing to do with any of this." August's face reddened.

Norabell said, "I want to know why another family didn't take me?"

"If another family had taken you, we wouldn't be talking like this now. We probably would have never known anything about your life. Any family that you would have lived with would probably have been a long ways away. Count your blessings that you are with true family."

Norabell put her hands in her lap. "Why did Momma take me? It was not her place to raise me. It was yours."

"Some questions are not easily answered, but Momma did more than most would have taken on themselves to protect you from shame."

Lottie came and stood beside August and Norabell. "I guess I'm the only one that can complete this time of confession and truth. Come with me."

Together they went to the bedroom, and Lottie pulled a chair beside the front of the chest. She turned the key and opened it. "I guess there's no need any more to try to hide the key. I'll leave it here. All secrets are now open for the family to see." She gently rubbed her hand over the edge of the open top. "It has held more than enough secrets in its time.

There were some surprises that I found in this chest myself. There I found a letter from my Momma's first husband while he was away fighting in the war." She smiled amidst her tears. "I was a plunderer like Norabell. I found that note when I was twelve. Until then, I never knew Momma was married before. She told me the whole story. There was also a letter from a man that saw her husband die, and he told her about how he talked about his love for her and his two children that were home. Two? I then asked her about a second child, and she told me about losing a daughter after her husband had died. To the fever, she said. It changed a lot of things between me and her after that. We talked more. She seemed like a different person. Secrets have a way of making a person lonely, I think. Truth should always bring people together. It sets you free."

Norabell and August took out the letters. August read the one from Tom. Norabell opened the one she never got to finish that day when she had almost been caught snooping in the chest.

She scanned down the page and found where she had left off.

I am sorry that I have disappointed you. If I could change it, I would. It would be hard

*not only for me but also for you and Papa.
I can't imagine how people would treat this
poor baby. I saw how it is when girls I
know have a child out of marriage. I'm
older and I should have known better. But
it's too late to cry over spilled milk. Help
me to know what to do. Pray I do the right
thing.*

August

Lottie closed the lid to the chest, and they
stood up. They walked into the other room.

Lottie went to the water bucket and got a
drink. She brought the dipper back and passed
it to August, and then to Norabell.

August slipped her hand into her bosom
and pulled out a piece of paper. "I kept a letter
of my own. It's one that I want Norabell to
read." She turned to Lottie. "It's the one that
you sent back to me in answer to the one that
Norabell just finished."

She turned to her daughter. "Do you want
to read it?"

Norabell swallowed and reached for the
letter. "Can I go outside and read by myself?"

"Go wherever you like. I understand your
need to be alone. I think it'll answer a few
questions for you."

Norabell left and sat by the creek on a stump.

My dearest daughter August,

Let me start by saying you have not disappointed me. Not really. I never told you but my firstborn was conceived in a lapse in judgment also. It did not make him any less loved or wanted. Thankfully, he was nothing like his Papa. He was kind and good and a wonderful son. I'll never forget the way he looked for this sister, Annie May, when she died in the flood. Talking about your oldest brother, Brody, brings me to say this. To have given him away would have felt like he had died to me. You may feel that you are not able to keep this child. Somewhere there is a man that will not care about your past, as Beck has been with me. He will love you no matter what. I want to take this baby as my own. I have planned all along to ask you if I could raise it. So much so, that I have added a little padding of my own as I walk through town. Just in the right places, and just a little more along as needed. Everyone thinks that I am with child. I never said I was, but neither did I deny it. Beck would walk away when someone mentioned my swollen belly. We never discussed it, but he knew where my mind had taken me. He's that kind of man. I didn't have to ask his permission. It was just as important to him that this baby come back to us, and I knew it. When you come home, this child is mine to everybody, including you, Maggie, and anyone that asks. The other children will just think they have another brother or sister. If it's a boy, I want to name him Beckly after your Papa. I never did get to name one after him. If it's a girl, she's to be called Norabell. I once had two friends, one was Nora and the other Bell. I don't know what happened to them after I moved from the mountains, but I've never forgotten them. Please don't let that teacher put the baby on the train. Bring it home.

Love,

Your Momma

Norabell wiped tears from her eyes and looked up. Across the creek stood PeNellie and her grandmother.

"We're leaving, my friend. I wanted to say goodbye. I was hoping you would be here at your Momma's."

Norabell stood up and walked closer to the creek. "I will miss you, and I'll never forget you."

"Nor I you. You never judged me. I see tears in your eyes. That makes me sad. My wish is that you never have a reason to cry again."

Norabell smiled. "These are actually happy tears. For a time I was sad, as I didn't know who I really was, but now I do. I'm the same person I always was. It doesn't matter my past. I'm Norabell. There is nothing I would change even if I could."

Mamia raised her arm into the air. "Times will change, but your happiness will only grow. I see many, many children." She laughed. "A long time, and lots of very good times in Dugan Holler."

They turned and climbed the hill. PeNellie turned before they were out of sight and waved.

Chapter 20

There was a headline across the Democrat Union that caught Beck's eye. He picked up a copy and carried it to the truck. The headline read Dawson Gray...A Free Man.   A scan through the article told him that the verdict of 'Guilty of Manslaughter' had been overturned. The jurors that had been persuaded to change their vote by the judge and the Carver's attorney had gone to a lawyer and told him what happened. He, in turn, went to Dawson, and he hired him to take the case. On behalf of the defendant, the attorney requested that the verdict be set aside and that Dawson be given a new trial.   They were said to support their cause by stating the ill advice given to the jury by the judge and the Attorney General that they would need to certainly make a verdict and not leave that day as a hung jury.

The new lawyer laid out a number of special requests that the defendant had asked that the jury be made known. That it was the law that a person could not order the defendant to quit using the road nor use force to stop him from doing so. That the defendant had every right to go down that road and that he had the right to remove the barrier that kept him from doing so. There was a complete list of failures of the court to advise the jury the laws the deceased had broken.

Beck skipped to the end. "Let it be noted that Dawson Gray was granted a new trial. However, The Attorney General moved that the Court order a nolle in this cause stating that there was insufficient evidence to convict and no new evidence had been discovered. Therefore, a nolle, stating they would not prosecute, was entered."

Beck put down the paper. "Well….that's that, I guess."

***

Lottie, August, and Norabell sat on the porch of the house in Dugan Holler.

"I say twins." August laughed.

"Shut your mouth. It's all she can do with a first baby to tend to one at a time. But I do say it's a girl." Lottie pulled out about eighteen inches of string. She leaned her head down and bit it off with her teeth.

"Do you believe that really works? Can a thread really tell what a baby will be?" Norabell cupped her swollen belly.

"It worked for me, and it worked for August according to Maggie."

August said, "It will be a girl. Norabell is as graceful as she can be. They say if it's a boy, she would be clumsy."

"Phooey. Not true. Which side do you lay on at night?"

Norabell raised her eyebrows and twisted back and forth. "I guess that would be my right side, but I think that's because I can lay my legs across Jake."

"Then it's a girl!" Lottie raised her finger to the sky.

August laughed. "But then I think I have noticed that Jake is gaining weight right along with Norabell. That means a boy."

"That weight gain is due to Momma's cooking since we moved back to Dugan Holler.

She feeds us every night since I told her I was carrying a baby."

"There goes that theory, Miss August," Lottie said.

Jake's momma said it was a boy because I've had almost no morning sickness. She said with her boys, she was never sick."

Lottie shook her head. "What does a mother-in-law know? The mother of the baby knows what she's having as does the pregnant woman's Momma, and I say it's a girl."

August cackled. "And who would that BE, Momma. You or ME? I say it's a boy?" She leaned over and pulled Norabell's dress up above her knees. "Look at the hair on that girl's legs. Growing like weeds those hairs are. Yep, a boy for sure."

Norabell jerked her dress back over her legs.

They both looked at Norabell. She laid back on the porch. "Just get it over with."

Lottie reached out her hand and Norabell took off the small band of metal that Jake had put on her finger the day they married. "I have never had this off my finger since the day we married. What if I don't want to take it off?"

Lottie shrugged her shoulders. "Then I guess you'll have to rely on all these other things we've been telling you."

It took several twists around her lightly swollen finger to dislodge the ring. Norabell handed it to her mother. "Let the ring and string tell me what I'm having." She laid back on the porch and raised up her shirt.

"Let me see that whole belly, young lady." August laughed.

Norabell blushed. "That is the whole belly, and you know it. I'm not as huge as the two of you try to make out. Twins, my foot."

Lottie slipped the ring onto the thread and held both ends in her right hand. She scooted a chair and leaned her arms over Norabell's belly. She lowered the ring to right below Norabell's belly button. It was still except for the light shaking of Lottie's hand. Ever so slowly, it began to move back and forth, then quickly changed to swing into small circles.

"It's a girl!" Lottie yelled.

"A girl. We'll have a granddaughter." August rocked back and forth as she laughed.

Lottie shushed them. "Wait a minute. It had stopped, and now it is moving again." This time it swung back and forth across her stomach. "After that she'll have a boy.....here it goes again."

The ring went back and forth again.

"Another boy."

"My, my. Here it goes again."   The ring circled in a large round circle.

"A girl."

Norabell raised up. "That's about enough. This could go on all day long."

They laughed.

"The old ring and string test, I see." Beck walked up and Jake was right behind him.

"It's a girl this time." Lottie piped up.

August started, "But, Jakes, there'll be……"

"Oh no you don't. You're not giving him any ideas about how many children we'll have. Don't you say a word."

Jake raised his eyebrows.

Lottie stood up and laughed. "Have a seat. It's time for Friday night get together for this family. I bartered for some sugar, and we're having teacakes tonight."

***

Everyone had left. Lottie and Beck sat down in the swing, and Beck moved it back and forth gently.

Beck put his arm over the back of the swing and pulled Lottie toward him. "This is the life. If I had of had time to plan our last years, this would have been just like I would have wanted."

Lottie leaned her head on Beck's shoulder. "I feel like all is right with the world. Even though there is a war out there. I have grandchildren that are leaving soon to go, yet I feel at peace. I am praying that they will be alright, and will come home safe. It's hard to believe they are grown enough to fight a war. They were barely in their teenage years when we left. I miss them. The only thing that would make this time better would be for everyone to move to Tennessee. It probably won't happen. They have their own lives."

Beck kissed the top of her head and got up. 'I'm going to bed."

"I think I'll sit here a bit and breathe the good clean air and listen to the owls hoot."

After he shut the door, Lottie blew out the lamp on the table beside the swing and sat in the darkness.

She traveled slowly through her entire life in her mind, pausing at hard times and let the tears fall. Other times, she would laugh and shake her head. She traveled from her childhood days in the mountains of Jackson County in North Carolina, her days in Cocke County, Tennessee, the struggles of life in the mill towns of Clifton, South Carolina and Morganton, North Carolina. Dugan Holler was the culmination of life that she had had no knowledge of from the beginning. Everything had happened without her foresight or consent. There was one in far greater control of the destiny of one's life. She realized it was a good thing. If she had been in control, or even knew what the next day would bring, it would not have ended as well as it had. Good times and bad times happen to all. The happenings are all laced together like Beck took the white oak strips and wove bottoms to the chairs that sat on the porch...up and down, back and forth. It was not easy surviving bad spells. All you can do is to carry on. The only other choice of a way out was to intentionally depart from life, and it was one that she could not understand...to leave by choice in the middle of troubles. If you chose that road, you would miss the good times that are bound to happen if you could but hold on.

Lottie stood and walked to the edge of the porch. The trees were outlined against the moonlit sky. A million stars twinkled all around.

"Thank you, Dugan Holler, for restoring my faith in the goodness of life. May it bring the same happiness to any other family that may own this land in the years to come."

Bibliography/Acknowledgements:

(1) Excerpt: Eleanor Roosevelt Papers.
      Teaching Eleanor Roosevelt, ed. by
      Allida Black, June Hopkins, et. al. (Hyde
      Park, New York: Eleanor Roosevelt
      National Historic Site, 2003).
      http://www.nps.gov/elro/teaching.htm
      [Accessed (August 2014)].

_____

(2) The Lawrence County Library and the
      Lawrence County Tennessee Archives.
      The Democrat Union on microfiche.

_____

(3) "One Man's Vison...One County's
      Reward", Kathleen Graham-Gandy,
      2013.

Made in the USA
San Bernardino, CA
29 December 2015